The Puddle Street Chronicles

The Puddle Street Chronicles

Alan Kelly

The Puddle Street Chronicles

Text copyright©2022 Alan Kelly
Cover©2022 Katherine Mabey

ISBN 978-1-8380247-8-9

British Library Cataloguing in Publication Data.
A catalogue record for this book is available from the British Library.

6 3 5 4 2

First Published in Great Britain
Hawkwood Books 2022

Printed and bound in Great Britain by CPI Group (UK) Ltd.
Croydon CR0 4YY

For my wonderful wife
Marie

1. *'FFFFFUUMPH!*

On a bright Saturday morning, full of summer, in a tidy little bedroom on Puddle Street, Sally Bunn slammed a book shut.

'Science....*sucks!*' she moaned, flopping onto her bed like an empty glove puppet.

And it's always the same. No matter how hard she tries to get her head around science subjects, especially physics, she never quite makes it. Funny thing though, on pretty much every other subject she's one of the smartest kids in school: gold stars, straight A's, academic awards, no problem. But science – forget it.

She was in such a tizz, she jumped when her phone dring-dringed. It was Toby from across the road.

'Yo, Bunn. It's the great Sprocket.'

Taking a deep breath, Sally eye-rolled the ceiling.

'I said Yo, Bunn. It's the great Sp--'

'...I heard you the first time, Toby.'

'Hey – you sound kind of fed-up?'

'That's because I *am* kind of fed up. It's all this exam stuff. I think my head is about to explode.'

Toby clucked his tongue in mock pity. 'Now that would be a bummer. I mean, blowing up a brain as big as yours.'

'Thanks, Toby. Really helpful that.'

'No probs,' Toby replied easily. '*And* I might also have a way of ditching your fed-up-ness.'

'Is that so?'

'It is so.'

'Go on, then. Start ditching.'

'It's Unc… I've never seen him so excited. I think he's got something extra-special up his sleeve today, and he wants us to help out.'

'Toby, I can't. It's ok for you. You'll pass everything as usual, you swine. But I'm really struggling *and* I really want to read a play for drama class.'

There was a pause. Sally bit her lip.

'Toby… you still there?'

'Course I am. I'm waiting for an answer – you in or out?'

'Oh I don't know.'

'You don't know what?'

'Did I not just explain, you big dope: class studies!'

'Gah, studies-schmudies, you'll nail it, Sal. You always do. Also, and I hope you don't mind me saying this, but you're probably the biggest swot in London.'

'Why would I mind you saying it, since it's true.'

'Well then, there you go, you can sort it out tomorrow, after karate class maybe. I'll even throw in a pizza with extra pepperoni and mushrooms. Because nothing, and I do mean nothing, is too good for my best mate. Although come to think of it, it's your turn for the pizza.'

Sally guessed all along Toby would persuade her, and in his usual smart-alecky way that's precisely what he did.

'Ok you win. Down in a mo,' she beamed, launching herself off her bed, yanking-on her favourite jeans and jacket and brushing her hair until it shone like a blond crash helmet. And before her mum could finish the words "….make sure you're home for tea…" she had already shot out the front door.

And there he was, skinny as a pencil, leaning against

a street lamp, with that clump of black hair shaped into spikes. Toby never quite got the hang of matching his clothes. And yet, even in that ghastly faded denim jacket and those crummy old combats (the awful green ones....yuck...) he still managed to look like he always did – seriously cool.

'Sorry for moaning earlier. It's these exams...you know.'

'Forget it.' Toby shrugged, shoving his hands into his pockets. 'Let's go see Unc.'

Ever since his parents died in a car crash when he was a baby, Toby had lived with his uncle at No 2 Puddle Street. And what a house to live in. It's hard to describe the Sprockets old place. What was once a grand London townhouse, now looked like it had been thrown together with building site left-overs. Think wonky doors, bumpy floors and lopsided walls, not to mention battered suits of armour, a genuine human skeleton *and* a super-cool pinball machine that still bing-bonged like crazy, and that was just the sitting room. Sally loved the place. She loved her own house too of course, all renovated and modern with lots of comfy chairs and carpets. And she totally adored her accountant dad and doting mum who knitted fluffy scarves and baked the best bread and butter pudding in England. But the Sprocket house was so very different.

And then there was Toby's uncle, the world famous Professor Arthur C. Sprocket, scientific mastermind, now retired. Sally liked the professor because he was so great at explaining complicated science stuff. There was also his dry sense of humour and the fact that he actually looked like a mad professor from one of those old 1950s sci-fi movies. On the other hand, since he hardly ever left his stuffy little lab, or saw natural daylight, he was completely useless at everyday stuff like ironing clothes or eating properly. In fact, if it wasn't for his nephew Toby, he would have cashed in his chips years ago.

They soon entered Toby's house and slammed the front door behind them.

'Toby…Sally, is that you?' the professor called from his lab, leaning back from his desk and pushing his glasses up onto his baldy head.

'Good morning, professor,' Sally called back, shucking her jacket onto the stair bannister that was covered with the usual stack of coats. 'Thank you for inviting me over.'

'Don't mention it, my dear. And I hope you will enjoy my little surprise later on. Oh, and don't forget, Toby… the cubbyhole?'

Sally threw a questioning look.

'Oh yeah. *The cubbyhole,*' Toby smiled. 'You'll get a real kick out of this.'

And so they galloped excitedly up the creaky stairs: clumpity-clump-clump-clump, only stopping when they reached a small door on the first landing.

'After you,' Toby said, pushing the door open and nodding towards a pitch-black threshold.

Sally peered in nervously at bunches of raggedy cobwebs swaying about like ghostly white hair.

'Can't you just tell me what it is?' she pleaded, in a whisper.

'No, no, you need to see it for yourself,' Toby insisted, half-pushing Sally through the doorway. 'And don't worry. We'll use our phones for light.'

Creeping and crawling through dust and clutter, they eventually reached the furthest corner of the cubbyhole.

'Now what?' Sally asked worriedly, desperately fighting the heebie-jeebies.

'Look there,' Toby said, pointing his phone towards a wall. 'Whatcha think of that?'

When her eyes adjusted to the half-light, Sally could see words gouged into the wall plaster.

Herbert Herring
Inky Blyster
1610

'Wow! Is that for *real?*' she marvelled, her eyes locking onto the names. 'I mean 1610? It's like…hundreds of years old.'

'At least…' Toby nodded. 'And yeah, it is for real.'

'How come you guys never noticed them before?' Sally said, drawing a finger inside the tracks of each letter.

'It was too well hidden.' Toby explained. 'Unc only found them when he pushed a box in here and accidently shifted a loose timber. And there it was. Anyway, enough of the ancient stuff. We still have a 21st century surprise waiting for us.'

Seconds later they were in the professor's congested little lab surrounded by a mishmash of gizmos and gadgets, blackboards covered in complicated equations, books on every subject under the sun, and a bank of computer screens that were perfect for gamming fun whenever Toby and Sally got the chance.

At the back of the lab something grabbed Sally's attention; a naked light bulb swung lazily back and forth over a covered bundle. She could hardly take her eyes off it.

'Ok, Unc. What's the big surprise then?' Toby asked, straining to see past his uncle.

'The *big surprise* happens to be my greatest ever invention!' the professor answered with a smile. 'And here it is! The wonderful, truly remarkable, Anti-Gravity Machine, Mark 5.'

With a great theatrical swoosh he pulled a heavy cotton sheet off the bundle, sending plumes of dust swirling through the air. All at once the most amazing hunk of techno-wizardry was right there in front of Toby and Sally. It looked like a sleek dodgem car made of semi-transparent plastic with a gleaming glass canopy on top. Crammed inside was a dazzling array of circuitry that blinked and sparkled like electronic jewels. Toby and Sally were instantly hooked.

'It looks fabulous, professor,' said Sally. 'Imagine! A machine that floats!'

'Wow Unc, it's totally *sick!*' Toby exclaimed, almost knocking his uncle over in a mad rush to climb on board.

'No-no-no,' the professor frowned. 'Not just yet.'

'B---'

'No buts! Before we can even begin the ignition procedure there are safety protocols and technical instructions to deal with first.'

'We *are* gonna try it though. I mean, to check that it actually floats in the air?' Toby said, flashing his extra-special sad face that always worked on his uncle.

'Of course you are – that's why you're here. And the sooner we get these few technical guidelines out of the way, the better. So, listen-up and pay attention.'

With his bags under his eyes looking darker and more bulging than usual, the professor launched into a tirade of scientific mumbo-jumbo.

'*Blah blah...* accentuate the flak bleurons...*blah blah...* reconflute the main conspungelator... *blabbidy blah blah...* close the canopy and...*blah blah...*re-charge the plunarkin batteries... finally then, you must select the correct binary code platotus *alongside* the 1337 HTTP airloopatrons...'

With a look of rapt indifference on their faces, and expecting at least a ten-minute oration, Toby and Sally were taken aback when the professor abruptly concluded the lecture.

'...and so to conclude. I would like to thank both of you for your participation, and especially for your attentiveness in this, the inaugural test run for the Mark 5.'

'Good grief, Unc. That was very nearly interesting.' Toby said cheekily. 'And now that we know all the technical thingies and floaty stuff, can we try it on for size?'

'Really... technical thingies and floaty stuff... *that's* what you heard?' said the professor, pinching the bridge of his nose. 'You know, Toby. Trying to hold your attention is a lot like trying to hold an octopus in a pair of underpants. But yes... you *may* sit inside while I configure the computer. On no account can you touch any of the controls.'

Sally was always an ace at observing things, so when the initial rush of excitement was over, she noticed a few disquieting details. First there was all those wires creeping out from the back of the Mark 5 like multicoloured snakes. There was also an unnerving sickly-sweet burning smell wafting-up from the bowels of the machine. And most worrying of all was a weird purring noise that sounded like a giant cat waiting to be stroked. She decided it best to say nothing. Besides, what could possibly go wrong in a tiny attic lab on boring old Puddle Street.

As Sally slid down into the cockpit, she noticed a mischievous grin widening across Toby's face. And when he pulled the glass canopy over – closing it with a dull clunk – she smacked his arm.

'Toby...please!'

'Please what?'

'Didn't you even *listen* to what your uncle said?'

'Jeez Sal. It's only the canopy.'

Just then the professor, flipping pages on a clipboard, returned.

'Okeydokey,' he began. 'It's almost time to get this show on the road. I just need to check a couple of details first. So can you step outside for a moment.'

'C'mon, let's move.' Sally said, pushing the canopy open.

However, just as they began to hoist themselves out, three seemingly harmless events occurred.

First: Toby's jacket snagged on the canopy latch, jerking them back down hard into their seats.

Second: the canopy toppled over and slammed shut!

Third: and most worrying of all – Sally's elbow flicked a big red switch. It sounded like the trigger of a gun being cocked.

Almost immediately a burst of shuddering jolts raced through the Mark 5. And even though, terrifyingly, it just got louder and louder, it was when thick blue smoke began swirling around the machine, that Toby and Sally began yelling and screaming and pulling at the canopy latch.

'It's stuck, its stuck!' Toby shouted. 'Help us, Unc! Help us!'

'Don't pull at it so hard!' the professor shouted back,

before he dived rugby-style to unplug the machine from the wall. Unfortunately, because he had already locked the plugs into the wall for safety, no amount of diving would save the day.

By that stage the machine was screeching like a beast in agony and for one horrible moment the professor thought the whole thing was about to explode. In a blind panic he fell to his knees, pulled his white coat over his head, and started screaming. Now the stage floor was rocking beneath them, and fragments of dust and plaster rained down like confetti. Just when the mad hullabaloo seemed to have reached its peak, a peculiar muffled noise spluffed through the attic....

*FFFFF***UUMPH*!'*

...it went, followed by a long eerie silence.

It took quite a while before the professor dared poke his head out from under his coat. When he did, all he found was a numbing silence and tendrils of blue smoke curling up into the ancient rafters. The strangest thing of all, however, was the total absence of the Mark 5?

'I-It must have moved somehow,' he mumbled, his bald head shining with sweat. 'Bound to happen with all that commotion.'

He searched through every nook and every cranny in every room throughout the house. But it was no use. The Mark 5 was nowhere to be found. Utterly distraught the professor sank to the floor and hugged his knees into his chest.

'Noooooooo, no-no-no-no!' he wailed miserably. 'I

have destroyed them. I've gone and destroyed the poor little blighters.'

The professor couldn't possibly have known it – but right at that very moment Toby and Sally were far from destroyed. In fact they were relatively safe and sound and about to embark on the most amazing adventure in the entire history of... well... pretty much everything!

2. 1610 AGAIN?

High above the freezing waters of the Thames two hungry seagulls were busy dive-bombing an old magpie for her precious cargo of scraps. The magpie spun, ducked, dipped and swivelled, but it was all to no avail. In the cold wintery light the skirmish spun-out to its only possible conclusion. Defeated and worn-out the old magpie drifted away across a sea of purple-grey rooftops.

Beneath one of those very rooftops a young chap was warming his toes by a roaring fire. He was house-minding his uncle's brand-new townhouse while he was away doing business in Scotland – and boys-oh-boys was that young chap enjoying every minute. A smile tugged at the corners of his mouth as he spread dollops of mustard on a wedge of pork pie his adoring mum had brought over earlier. He hungrily scoffed it down, and with his belly contentedly full he settled back for a nice little after-snack snooze.

Just on the verge of a pleasant *z Z* z *Z* Z a peculiar noise from upstairs startled him. It was so peculiar it made him jump right out of his chair. Stuffing the last chunk of pie into his mouth he grabbed a fireside poker and crept silently across the sitting room floor. Keeping absolutely still and settling his ear at the edge of the door, he listened for all his worth.

Meanwhile, high up in the cold dark attic an amazing event was taking place…

'FFFFFUUMPH!'

...a noise went, followed by a long eerie silence.

Toby and Sally, their faces locked in a noiseless scream and their hands gripping the control panel, could hardly breathe. It took some time before their terror-stricken eyes even dared to look around.

Toby swallowed. 'I-I think it's over now, Sally?' he said, as he unlocked the canopy, which annoyingly opened without a hitch this time.

'Hey Unc, sorry about that,' he announced chirpily as he stepped out from the machine. 'But all's well that ends well, eh Unc... Unc...?'

Toby's voice dwindled away into a strange inexplicably dark room. And except for a haze of blue smoke swirling around his ankles, there was nothing else there?

'He must have hightailed it downstairs with fright!' he suggested, hunching his shoulders towards Sally.

Sally wasn't so sure.

Looking around she hardly recognized the place. Instead of the usual jumble of science equipment there was nothing but silence. Even the attic door, ordinarily crooked with age, looked brand new and straight as an arrow. Equally strange was the smell of new paint and fresh cut timber – not smells Sally usually associated with the Sprocket household.

'Toby, this is *so* not right,' She whispered. 'I mean... where has everything gone... all the professor's stuff. He couldn't have moved it all out so fast?'

'No,' said Toby, slowly. 'He definitely could not. Let's hope we haven't destroyed it all.'

'I beg your pardon...*we?*' Sally huffed. 'How come its *we* all of a sudden?'

'Ok then... *I,*' Toby said. 'Let's hope *I* haven't destroyed it all. Happy now?'

By then Sally wasn't really listening. The emptiness of the attic was beginning to scare her... a lot.

'It's just *so* not right,' she repeated, unable to keep the fear out of her voice. 'Don't you feel it as well, Toby?'

'Feel what?'

'The strangeness. Weird, huh?'

'Yeah, weird.' Toby said, scratching his head. 'But... maybe we're just in a different room.'

'Well, you live here. what other room *could* it be?'

Clearly flustered, Toby ignored that question. 'Let's keep going,' he said. 'just in case.'

'What do you mean, just in case! Just in case what?'

'Sal. What do you want me to say. Just in case Unc has set us up for a big joke or something.'

'Yes, of course. I never thought of that. It could all be a big joke.'

Moving out towards the landing, Sally gripped Toby's arm with a vice-like grip. 'What's-wrong-what's-wrong?' she hissed when he stopped unexpectedly.

'Shhh!' Toby whished. 'Can't you hear that?'

'I can't hear anything?'

'Precisely!' Toby said. 'There's nothing... not even traffic noise?'

'Maybe our ears were damaged by all that racket in the machine?' Sally suggested.

'Yeah, maybe. But how come we can hear each other perfectly, and we're whispering?'

Moving out from the lab they began making their way down the stairs. Puzzling discrepancies were everywhere: no dust, no cobwebs, and most confusingly, no creaking floorboards. Peering between the wooden railings down into the hallway, they noticed it was spotlessly clean – even the perpetual stack of coats was missing from the bottom banister.

Finally, when they reached the bottom of the stairs they were hugely relieved to see, through a narrow opening in the sitting room door, silhouettes of flame dancing across the wall. Toby sensed the presence of someone just inside the door.

'Phew!' he whispered, mock-wiping his brow and pointing his thumb at the door. 'He's hiding on the other side… let's give him a little surprise of our own.'

All at once they bounced into the sitting room, ready for a big laugh at the professor's expense.

'Ok Unc, what's the big i…de….' Toby's voice trailed off into a stunned silence when, in place of his uncle, they were confronted with a scruffy young chap holding a poker over his head.

The three youngsters stood gawping at each other until the chap brandishing the poker decided he should shout loudly at the two strange intruders. Unfortunately he forgot about the food in his mouth.

'Whof-da-hef-arf-youf-twof?' he spluttered, shooting fragments of half-chewed pork pie in all directions.

'Do you *mind!*' Sally said disgustedly, brushing pieces of pie from her face and clothes. 'That's just gross.'

Choking down the remains of the pie, the scruff aggressively snorted.

'I said, who the hell are you two?' backing-up his enquiry with a swish of the poker.

By that stage Toby was in no mood for larking about.

'Who the hell are *we*?' he yelled back. 'Who the hell are *you,* anus breath. And what are you doing in my uncle's house?'

'*Your* uncle's house!' the scruff exclaimed, his eyes bulging out like golf balls. 'You're mad – completely mad, the pair of you! Be off with you while you still can. My friend.... I mean my *friends* will be here at any minute....my *four* friends, that is. A-And then you'll find out what's what.'

Although scared, the scruff sensed he was in no immediate danger but merely dealing with a simpleton and his crazy female companion. Further poker-wielding should scare them away no problem.

Toby was evidently thinking likewise as he squared up aggressively to the scruffy git. Sally was distraught and could see trouble fast approaching.

'Please Toby,' she urged him, close to tears. 'This can't be your house. Let's just go.'

'Sally, will you listen for a minute,' Toby pleaded. 'What if we were dazed or knocked unconscious by all that shaking in the machine? And what if Unc has gone to get a doctor – and this scruffy git *and his cronies!* he shouted accusingly towards the scruff, '...are in the process of clearing the place out.'

'Toby, pleaseeee. Look around. Everything is clean, and nothing is old. Also where's all your stuff? It would take a year to clear all that alone. And when was the last time you saw a fire in your front room? Chimneys around London has been blocked-up for years.'

Toby looked at the bare walls and all the other anomalies Sally had pointed out. She was spot-on: this couldn't be his house.

'Ok, maybe you're right, Sal. Maybe we should leave.'

And with that, Toby grudgingly gave-in and began to back out slowly to the hallway.

Deeply relieved, the scruffy git rushed past them to open the front door. That was when he noticed how unusual these nutters truly were. For a start their clothes were most peculiar, and the girl's golden hair looked like spun silk. Plus she was wearing trousers, and that definitely wasn't right. Strangest of all was how clean and perfumy they smelt – which could only mean one thing. They must have had an all-over wash recently, and it wasn't even Christmas.

'Mores the point,' he said to himself. *'How did they get in here in the first place?'*

As soon as the intruders were seen off, the scruff locked the front door and set about checking security arrangements throughout the house. The last place he checked was the attic – although he couldn't imagine how any burglar could break into the house by that route.

You can well imagine his surprise when he discovered the weirdest looking contraption he had ever seen just sitting right there in the shadows.

'Hells bloody bells!' he gasped, creeping around the bizarre looking thingamajig. 'How did *that* get up here?'

The more he thought about it the more convinced he was that the contraption must belong to his uncle. Most likely he had presumed his dim-witted nephew would never go snooping around a gloomy attic, and therefore his contraption would remain safe and unnoticed. And if it wasn't for the appearance of those super-clean loonies, his uncle would have been dead right.

Outside, a bolt of lightning split the sky followed by a rumbling explosion of thunder. It shook the house and continued to rumble and grumble like a narky giant. A storm had declared its intentions, which was reason enough for the scruff to put the whole baffling affair behind him. So off he scampered downstairs to his nice

little sitting room and his nice little fire.
But still, that contraption….?

3. DEEP DO-DO

Toby and Sally stepped out across the threshold into a strange foggy world they did not recognise. They jumped two feet in the air when the door slammed behind them, followed by a loud ker-clunking of locks, bolts and latches. It was daytime, but spreading-out in front of them in all directions was a blur of grey smoking chimneys. Even the air smelled funny – like old onions and stinky poo.

'What's going on...' said Toby, looking at a row of new houses with their snow-white walls and glistening windows. He though he knew that part of London like the back of his hand, but this place looked ghostly and other-worldly.

Sally rubbed her eyes as if she was seeing things.

'Well, it *sorta* looks like Puddle Street... doesn't it?'

'Yeah... *sorta*.' Toby answered, though struggling to understand where the traffic, the road markings and the footpaths were gone to.

'But if it *is* Puddle Street, then where's my house?' Sally said. 'And if it *isn't* Puddle Street, then where are we?'

Next to where they were standing, pretty much where Sally's house might have been, was a fenced-off field dotted with clumps of briars and nettles. At a corner of the field a flock of nervy sheep were eyeballing the newcomers. A flash of lightening and a kaboom of thunder collapsed around them, like a bomb going off. The sheep launched into a mad charge, crashing and banging and falling over each other in blind terror. Toby and Sally were so confused they just stood there like statues.

'Let's try that wall,' said Toby, pointing. 'We should be able to see something we recognize from there.'

The wall was just low enough for them to climb. Holding each other for balance they stretched their necks to scan the surrounding cityscape. It looked almost normal, but normal in a strange *ab*-normal sort of way.

'What the heck...' Sally said, shaking her head. 'I mean, what the bloody *heck...*'

There was no Millennium Wheel, no Big Ben or Tower Bridge – and the sky, all ashy and overcast, looked like the bleakest of bleak winter days: which confused them even more, since it was supposed to be the middle of July.

'Toby. This is getting freaky,' said Sally, staring again at the spot her family home should be. 'I mean, *really* freaky?'

'I-I know, Sal,' Toby stuttered. 'But it could be some kind of weird trick or something, or...or... oh hell, Sal, I dunno. I really don't?'

'That's it then – time for GPS,' Sally declared, pulling out her phone and jumping down from the wall.

Inexplicably, after flusters of tapping, shaking, and dialling, Sally's phone was totally dead.

'This is so weird,' she said, staring at the screen. 'Except for my old texts and photos, there's nothing.'

'What the... mine too?' said Toby, waggling his phone over his head in an effort to locate a signal. 'Well one thing's for certain,' he continued. 'We can't hang around here all day waiting for our phones to start working. We need to find the real Puddle Street and figure out what's happening.'

'Ok, let's do that then. But eh... in what direction *is*

Puddle Street?'

Pursing his mouth, Toby looked one way, then another, and then back again. 'I'm not a hundred per cent sure. But... this way, I guess?'

'You guess! You're not a hundred per cent sure, though?'

'No, Sal. I'm not. But it's a direction that looks right.'

'O-kaaay...' Sally shrugged. 'Right now though, I don't really care. I just want to get as far away from this place as possible.'

Unsure of exactly where they were going, they took to their heels in an effort to find at least one familiar sight that might help them. In their haste to get away, however, they failed to notice the shiny new plaque on the corner of the last house. It read **PUDDLE STREET** in big black letters.

Everything they knew seemed to have vanished. Instead of familiar bustling streets, they found narrow alien streets crammed with buildings that looked impossibly bigger on the top than on the bottom. The drone of London traffic was also missing – in fact there wasn't a single car, bus or motorbike to be seen? There was plenty of horses and carts and horse droppings, but that was it. Events rapidly went from ordinary weird to *extra*ordinary weird. Strangest of all were crowds of peculiar looking people dressed in peculiar clothes – all carrying-on and walking about as if everything was ok. And as soon as they clapped eyes on Toby and Sally, they sniggered, or stared open-mouthed, or started shouting for them to go back to wherever they came from.

'Why are we stopping?' Sally asked anxiously when Toby came to a sudden stop. 'Going by the dagger-looks we're getting I don't think we should hang around here for too long.'

Toby's attention was miles away. '...don't those streets look familiar – the ones shooting away from that pillar in particular. Don't you think it looks a bit like Charing Cross?'

'Yeah-yeah-sure-whatever,' Sally said all at once. 'Either way we should get out of here, like right now.'

'...and if we *are* near Charing Cross---'

'Toby. You *do* hear me talking. Right?

'...I think we should go this way?'

'At last! Let's get going then.'

Heading eastwards, and hugging the shadows as much as possible for safety, they rushed along lanes, alleys and backstreets, all of which lead exactly nowhere. Still they ran and ran, hoping against hope to find something, anything, that might help them to find their way home. Minutes or maybe even hours later, they couldn't really tell by that stage, they stopped to catch their breath.

'This is no use, Toby,' said Sally, her heart thumping madly. 'Maybe we should just turn back and start again?'

'Yeah ok...maybe... ' Toby said, swivelling his terrified eyes left and right and up and down. 'But let's keep going for a little bit more.'

Not long after that, just when they were on the verge of turning back, they heard a commotion ahead.

'Hear that?' said Toby, taking a few hesitant steps forward 'There's definitely something happening around that next corner.'

And sure enough, seconds later, they literally stumbled out onto a busy marketplace jam-packed with stalls and people and creaking overloaded wagons.

'Pe-uuuuUU!' Sally coughed, when a thousand ghastly smells charged up her nose. 'How can they *breathe* in this stuff?'

'Talk about pong central…' said Toby, from behind the jacket sleeve pressed over his nose and mouth.

Becoming acclimatised to the sights and smells of the market, they clambered onto nearby steps to look around. Out of nowhere, like a sluggish landslide, a scrum of brawling men tumbled into the open from a nearby ale house. Tussling, swearing, and wrestling, they threatened anyone who even dared to look in their direction. For two 21st century youngsters it was like a live performance of a nightmare – except the actors were real people and Toby and Sally were a very scared audience.

'I can't stand much more of this,' Sally declared, tears welling in her eyes. 'If only we knew what's happening? Do you think we're hallucinating or something?'

Toby stared across the bobbing heads of the people. 'Let's try the other side. It's not so packed over there.'

Dizzy with confusion they held hands and pushed their way through the heaving crowds. And even though they had nothing worth stealing – apart from some loose change – more than once they felt thieving little fingers dipping into their pockets. *Stay calm, stay calm, stay calm,* Sally repeated silently to herself as out-and-out panic threatened to engulf her.

Just as they reached the far side of the market a freakishly heavy shower collapsed across the city. For Toby and Sally it was the worst possible thing that could happen. It felt like the rain was attacking them, holding them back. Freezing and drenched they persisted with their search through fast-emptying streets. It wasn't long until a completely exhausted Sally had had enough.

'Toby, stop…' she ordered between gasps of chilly air. 'This is getting dangerous and ridiculous.'

'We don't have time for stopping, Sally. In case you haven't noticed, it's getting dark, and we still need to find

Puddle Street. Once we get there, Unc will make us supper and then---'

'....oh, for heaven's sake, Toby.' Sally snapped in frustration. 'Don't you get it? Your uncle won't be making us supper or tea or anything else. Surely you know what's going on here.'

'What are you talking about *going on here?* There's nothing *going on here.* We're lost, that's all. Lost. Or maybe it's a huge film set or some kind of theme park? O-Or maybe---'

Grabbing Toby by the arm, Sally stared into his face.

'...really, Toby? Maybe this-maybe that! What about maybe we've travelled back in time. What about *that* maybe?'

Even though the petrifying truth had been emerging street-by-street and brick-by-brick, Toby's mind refused to accept what was happening.

'No-no-no, there has to be a more logical explanation,' he said shakily. 'Time travel is baloney. We're just lost, that's all, lost and--'

Sally stamped her foot. '...goddammit, Toby. We are not just lost, and pretending otherwise is stupid,' she railed. 'Open your eyes won't you. We are in the past. The PAST. I haven't the foggiest idea how it happened. But somehow we have fallen back through time. And right now, instead of ignoring that fact, we need to know *when* and *where* we are?'

'I know, but... '

'---but nothing, Toby.' Sally cut-in again. 'We have to ask the first person who doesn't look like an axe murderer – where we are. We don't have a choice.'

Toby was in a daze. Surely Sally was wrong – surely this was some sort of illusion? A trick of the mind? The cold rain continued falling. His head dropped.

'Oh my god, you're right, Sal. I know you are. And it's all my fault. Messing around in that machine had something to with bringing us here… to the past. I caused this whole horrible thing to happen.'

Sally sighed heavily.

'Toby…you are not to blame, neither of us are. It's just some mad friggingly weird accident.'

'It doesn't matter what you call it, Sally. It's still my fault. Mine and mine alone. If I hadn't messed with that canopy---'

'Hellooooo… Earth calling Toby! Like… who was it hit the red switch? Me. And who was it made that stupid machine in the first place? Your uncle! Not you… YOUR UNCLE! So can we drop the self-pitying nonsense and try to get this mess sorted.'

Sally's words were like a cold shower. Toby lifted his chin.

'Yes…. Yes… of course. You're right,' he sighed. 'I so needed to hear that.'

Sally smiled. 'Not half as much as I did, Toby. Believe me.'

For a few minutes they stood there shivering in silence and hugging each other. And as the swirling rain intensified they knew with absolute certainty their old life had been scrubbed out of existence. They had no choice but to live with the strangeness and the wrongness of this new life. And somehow, come hell or high water, try to fix it.

'We really should get going,' Toby said eventually. 'Like you say, the sooner we find out where we are, the better.'

As it happened they were a few yards from an Inn. On cue a door flew open and a burst of yellow light poured across the wet street. A man (who didn't look like an axe murderer) staggered out. Sally took her chance.

'Excuse me, mister,' she called, rather louder than she intended.

'I mean, *sir,*' she began again. 'I'm sorry to intrude, but I was wondering if you could help us?'

Through a gale of alcoholic breath the man shouted his disapproval.

'No money for beggars! No money for beggars! Get away from me, now.'

'No sir, we don't want money,' Toby interjected smilingly. 'We're strangers in London and wondered if you might tell us where we are? We're lost, that's all.'

Through bleary eyes the man scrutinized his inquisitors.

'Hmm, I suppose you do look like out-of-towners,' he conceded grudgingly. 'So then. This is Ludgate Hill, my lad. That's Lud... gate... Hill.'

'Ludgate! Thank you very much, sir.' Sally said politely. 'You are most kind. There is one other thing, though. We were wondering like, what *year* it might be? I mean here... in Ludgate... Hill?'

With a wobble and a blink, the man stood still.

'What blasted year is it,' he shouted. 'Why, its 1610 of course. What other blasted year could it be?'

Grumbling like a bear the man staggered away through the rainy night: 'Humph, never heard such hogwash... what blasted year is it!'

Toby and Sally stared at each other: *1610... 1610!* The words bounced around their frightened heads. Everything they ever knew was really gone.

'That's it then. That really---is---it,' Toby exclaimed, shaking his head and staring wide-eyed at the ground. 'We have actually travelled back in time to 1610.'

As if to hammer the point home, a salvo of thunder

and a spiky bolt of lightning slashed the sky.

Sally looked up at the dark smouldering heavens. 'And you know what else this means?'

Toby rubbed his eyes. 'Sal. I don't think I *want* to know what else this means?'

'It means we've got to get back to that house, remember earlier... the little scruffy guy? Because that house has got to be No 2 Puddle Street!'

Toby gawped with a sudden realisation. 'Wow – you're right. Which is where the machine is. And like, if it brought us here, it has to bring us home as well. We need to get back there.'

'One thing, Toby. There's a good chance we'll have to throw ourselves at the mercy of the little scruffy guy.'

'Yeah, and if he tries to stop us, we'll fight our way in.'

'Wha... don't even *think* about fighting. I mean, don't even *think* about thinking about it. It's the dumbest thing I've ever heard!' Sally said fiercely.

'But Sal, we have to get back into that machine!'

'I do know that, Toby. But violence – not gonna happen. Like, what if we fight our way in and discover the machine has been *moved?* And what happens if we get arrested for assault, or something else we haven't even thought about. What then, eh? I'll tell you what then. We'll be up shit creek without a paddle *or* a boat.'

Toby relented: 'Excellent points, Sal. I wasn't thinking straight. Fighting with the scruff is not a good plan.'

'Abso-bloody-lutely it's not. We need to keep him sweet... lick his boots... become his slaves if that's what he wants. So long as it gets us back into that machine, we do whatever is needed.'

'Right. Agreed. Let's get started.'

All at once Sally stopped. 'Hold it...I've just thought of something else.'

'Please Sal, no more something-elses.'

'No Toby, listen. This is serious.'

'I *am* serious.'

'Where is Puddle Street?' Sally asked tentatively. 'I mean, I can't remember. Can you?'

Toby thought for a moment. 'Well no, not exactly,' he shrugged. 'But I don't see how that's going be a problem. It's not like we're trying to find another planet. We simply ask for directions. How hard can it be to find a whole street?'

As it worked out it was next to impossible to find a whole street, or at least the street they so desperately wanted. Not a single person knew *or* had ever even heard of Puddle Street.

'You listen to me, young fellow,' a gnarly old man with rheumy eyes protested. 'I've lived in London all my life and I never knowed of such a place called Puddle Street. And if I never knowed it, it don't exist.'

'But sir, we were there just a couple of hours ago... in a house... on Puddle Street.'

The old man hunched a shoulder dismissively. 'If that's the case you were either drunk or you're a dunderhead, or both.'

Sally pulled Toby aside. 'Toby, I think I've figured out why no one has heard of Puddle Street.'

'Yeah?'

'Remember that field opposite the houses – and how the houses looked newly built?'

'Right, and?'

'That's the reason nobody has heard of it. The street is so new it hasn't been given a name yet, like officially.'

'You know what, Sal. That's the only explanation that

makes any sense.'

'I think so.'

'Ok then. We need to get ourselves to the Thames.'

Sally scrounged her face. 'And that will help us, how?'

'Think about it. It's the one thing, perhaps the only thing we should be able to recognize in 1610. At the very least it will be flowing in the same direction.'

Sally face broke into a knowing smile. 'Of course – which will help us get our bearings, hopefully enough to find Puddle Street.'

'Correcto-mundo!' Toby beamed.

'That's an excellent strategy… for tomorrow! But right now we need something for tonight. I mean, it's getting darker and wetter. And we need food and shelter.'

'I was thinking about that,' Toby said, grimacing. 'Especially the food part.'

When the temperature suddenly dropped and the dreaded prospect of sleeping outdoors again was becoming a reality, whole new kinds of fear swept over them. Time was rushing along, the rain kept falling, and great piles of darkness filled the streets. And still they hadn't the foggiest idea what to do except stumble ahead and hope for the best. Eventually, shivering and sweating, they arrived at the mouth of an alley. In a far corner stood a terrace of derelict buildings. Rainwater tumbled down from a rusty drainpipe. They gulped at it heartily.

'Look, Toby. Over there,' Sally exclaimed, pointing towards a stone archway covered in ivy. 'I know it looks creepy, but it also looks dry.

Galloping through the icy drizzle they quickly found themselves under the heartening cover of a stone archway. Panting and shivering and flapping their arms round their shoulders, they almost died of fright when they noticed swirly shadows crawling around the walls like angry snakes.

They were not alone.

Pale scrawny men dressed in dun coloured rags were crouched over a glowing brazier stirring a pot of something steamy. Swivelling their heads they stared at Toby and Sally with dead eyes. Two of the men got to their feet and lazily shuffled towards the entrance of the archway. Toby and Sally exchanged a worried look. Sally gestured to leave. But Toby had other ideas. Cold and hunger (especially hunger) pushed him to the edge of carefulness.

'Sup guys,' he smiled. 'Shitty weather yeah!'

'What the...' Sally gasped, giving Toby a sharp look.

'Don't worry, Sal. I've got this,' Toby whispered through the corner of his mouth. 'We need to get food into our bellies. It'll be simp.'

'The only *simp* around here is you.' Sally hissed through clenched teeth.

'Sally... dry in here, wet out there... and that pot smells delicious.'

'No, it doesn't!' Sally urgently corrected him. 'It smells like boiled sick. I say we leave right now.'

Unfortunately by then, words couldn't be stopped flying out of Toby's mouth.

'Yummm, smells delish, guys,' he continued, his nostrils flaring at the steamy aroma. 'And hey, I know what you're thinking. You're thinking who are these weirdos and what do they want, amiright? Well, put your minds at ease. We're just two hungry strangers who wouldn't say no to a drop of your wonderful stew. And by the way, love the threads. If the caveman look ever takes off, you'll be in.'

Sally was aghast. 'Toby, have you completely lost your marbles?'

'News flash, Sal. Humour is timeless. I know what I'm doing. Trust me, ok. It's all part of my masterplan.'

'Masterplan! What *are* you talking about?'

'…just play along, yeah.'

'So guys…' Toby merrily continued. 'How's about letting us warm our backsides, eh?'

The men looked at each other quizzically, and then exploded into cackling laughter.

'I'll take that as a no, then,' Toby smiled. 'Hey, no probs! We'll just hang here until---'

Before Toby could finish, all hell broke loose. In a flash the men by the entrance (and some by the stew pot) were on their feet and lunging forward. In the blink of an eye Toby was pinned to the ground, and Sally's arm was pinioned behind her back. A stinging slap across the face silenced her screams.

Expertly restrained, the terrified teenagers could do nothing but watch in dread as a hooded figure slowly emerged from the shadows. It was a hunched older man, so filthy and smelly a gallon of soapy water would have struggled to wash the dirt off him. Leaning heavily on a crutch he stood over Toby and glared at him with cold cyborg eyes.

'So, you wants to warm yer backside, eh?' he said in a rasping voice. 'Well, ole Tab Dungworth will soon warm it up for you, don't you worry.'

To howls of mocking laughter Dungworth hacked up a gob of phlegm, slushed it around his mouth for added effect, and dribbled it onto Toby's cringing face.

'Ugggggh! You filthy pig…' Toby yelled, close to barfing and struggling like crazy.

'Aye, I could well be described as a pig,' Dungworth

sneered. 'But you're the one on the end of a spit!' And yet more howls of cackling laughter echoed around the archway.

When he rifled through the prisoner's pockets, Dungworth's face went stiff with anger when he saw Toby's strange coins.

'What's this supposed to be?' he roared, kicking Toby in the ribs for a speedy response. 'There had better be some proper cash or you're both for the chop.'

As soon as it was confirmed that no proper cash was to be had, Toby and Sally were ordered to stand up.

'Right then,' Dungworth growled. 'We'll have the clothes off yer backs instead.'

'No, no, please, you can't do this….!' Sally squealed. 'Please, you can't take my jacket. My mum bought it for me… take your hands off! Take your hands off!'

Biting her trembling lip, Sally looked over at Toby. At that exact moment they both understood that if they did nothing they would soon be dead ducks. Random scenes from karate class zoomed into Sally's brain – defence and attack played and re-played. But this was no school karate class: this was a live or die situation.

It was time to act, and there would be no second chances. To stand any chance of getting her moves right, Sally would have to be perfectly positioned.

'Damn it, girl – get a move on!' Dungworth roared, his voice crackling with rage.

'I'm trying to…' Sally whimpered. 'Please be patient, sir.'

With a knife pointing straight into her face, Sally raised a foot to open a shoelace. She pretended to topple over. On impulse her captor's hand shot out to steady her.

That was all she needed.

In a slick well-practiced move, Sally leaned slightly

to one side and kicked upwards, ramming her foot hard into her captor's belly. He instantly collapsed in wheezing agony. And before he had even hit the ground, Sally caught Dungworth between the eyes with a well-aimed elbow. He yelped in agony, staggered backwards, and joined his compatriot on the ground.

Remembering his own karate classes, Toby was busy side-kicking one goon in the forehead, and a second one even harder in the chest. Squealing like wounded mice they toppled over in a semi-conscious heap. With the element of surprise well and truly gone, the remaining men were preparing to charge with knives drawn.

'Follow me, Sally!' Toby yelled, grabbing their stuff and catapulting out the archway.

Old Tab Dungworth, bruised and battered, wasn't finished just yet. Never before had a victim humiliated him so. He hobbled after the escapees roaring and shouting.

'Thieves! Robbers! Foreigners! They stole our food! They stole our food!'

A handful of local men, lured by his ranting and raving, lazily gathered around.

'I have a silver penny for whoever captures one of those thieving foreigners!' Dungworth declared, raising a fistful of coins. 'What do you say to that?'

The mere mention of hard cash transformed the lazy locals into a baying mob. Easy money was not to be sniffed at, and since the rain had stopped, hunting foreigners was just the ticket. Whooping and howling they broke into separate groups and charged away in search of their prey.

With hearts thumping and lungs bursting, Toby and Sally were pelting along a maze of back alleys and side-streets. Eventually, unable to run no further, they flung themselves into a corner like a pair of exhausted puppies.

'Toby.... about your....masterplan....' Sally babbled. 'Didn't work out... too brilliantly.... did it?'

Since Toby was busy almost-dying, it took a while before he could answer.

'Ok... maybe it wasn't.... the greatest call ever.... Or else... they just couldn't take a joke....'

4. EVEN DEEPER DO-DO

Huffing and puffing to catch his breath, Toby casually looked over Sally's shoulder. His heart immediately sank. At the far end of the dark street four men were nosing and sniffing around like hungry sharks. Straightaway Toby recognized them: they were Dungworth's men from the archway. Anxiously he looked about for a way of escape. Unfortunately there was no easy way out.

'Oh-oh,' he said, leaning back into the shadows.

'Oh-oh-what?' Sally asked fearfully, her eyes darting in the direction of Toby's stare.

'We're not out of the woods just yet, Sal. Look…'

Sally shivered with dread. 'Oh God no… although, wait!' she whispered, pulling Toby further into the shadows. 'They haven't seen us… we might be ok.'

Unfortunately, from the corner of his eye, a particularly nasty looking brute with straggly hair caught sight of his quarry.

'There they be… there be the foreigners!' he yelled, pointing furiously and waving a cudgel.

Although his fellow brutes cheered excitedly, they didn't forget how much pain these particular foreigners could inflict. So instead of a direct attack they decided instead to launch a salvo of rocks, sticks, and stones from a safe distance.

Toby and Sally were managing to dodge the bombardment, when Toby noticed a bundle of rags winging its way towards them. Except it wasn't a bundle of rags – it was the rotting carcass of an extremely large dead rat. Sidestepping the incoming missile Toby watched transfixed as it hit Sally square on the back of her head. It burst open on impact, scattering hundreds of twitching maggots.

'Aiiiieeeeeeeee!!' Sally screamed, desperately flapping maggots from her hair and her face. 'Get-em-off, get-em-off, get-em-off!'

Her yelping and flapping was so funny it sent the attackers into fits of hysterical laughter. Despite that lull in the attack, Toby knew the situation would inevitably turn nasty again. It was time to take the bull by the horns, so Toby selected a rock the size of a cricket ball, rubbed it on the side of his trouser-leg and began tossing it from hand to hand.

'Oi, you!' he shouted at the yob who had thrown the rat carcass.

'Prepare to meet thy doom.'

'Wha... doom? W-What's he on about, lads?' the yob asked his pals, a trembling smirk on his face.

Marking his target, Toby narrowed his eyes and commenced a short loping run. Such weird behaviour seriously unsettled the attackers, who were already scrambling back from a clearly deranged foreigner.

'Y-You're crazy you are... stay back, *stay back!*' they shouted.

Toby wasn't for staying back: he was for bowling a deadly in-swinging bouncer with every ounce of his strength. A nano-second later the rock was arching gracefully through the air before hitting home with pinpoint accuracy... *clunk*... right between the eyes of the yob. His buddies watched in horror as he wobbled for a second or two, and then crumpled to the ground as if his very bones had been sucked from his body.

Toby and Sally grabbed the opportunity to

counterattack with a ferocious volley of rocks, sticks, and stones. Noses were flattened, ears were squashed, and heads were thwacked. The yobs certainly were not expecting such fierce resistance and made a hasty retreat.

'Right – that's our chance,' Toby yelled – and from somewhere they found the strength to run further and further into the heart of the old city.

Finally, exhausted beyond belief, they staggered behind a graveyard wall and collapsed. Too tired to be scared, they just lay there in a breathless heap. Eventually, when she found the energy to sit up, Sally picked the last of the maggots from her hair.

Suddenly she stiffened.

'I do *not* believe this!' she said in a small voice. 'There's more of those guys. The place is crawling with them.'

Pulling back into the shadows Toby narrowed his eyes and scanned the area. And sure enough, not twenty yards away, six men were standing around a fire next to a ramshackle old barn.

'Phew, it's not them!' he said. 'I think we're ok. But still, it's probably best if we get away from here.'

'No Toby, I can't move another inch.' Sally droned, her voice as weary as her body felt. 'If they decide to attack – let them. They'll be doing me a favour.'

The evening was rapidly turning into a chilly night, when the men unexpectedly started packing-up as if preparing to move out. For a pair of exhausted half-starved twelve year olds, the sight of a warming fire and a barn filled with straw looked like heaven. Unfortunately, just before leaving, the last man began stamping out the fire.

'Quick. We need to get to that fire,' said Toby, cursing their luck and dashing out as soon as the coast was clear.

While Toby fell to his knees and began blowing at the smouldering embers, Sally rushed around gathering as much dry tinder as possible,

'Please-please-light!' Toby begged between puffs. 'Just a spark, that's all we need.'

The fire was all but extinguished. But just when Toby was about to give up, the embers miraculously blazed back to life – and with a ready supply of kindling they soon had a nice cosy fire going. Sally also discovered something else the men left behind.

'Four potatoes – and I think, a turnip?' she declared holding the veggies up for inspection. 'How do we work these? Do we just eat them or what?'

'Search me,' said Toby, staring confusedly.

Sally chanced a nibble of turnip. 'Yuck...fthew...disgusting!' she spat: whereupon a further examination of the turnip followed.

'Heat cooks stuff, right?' Sally said eventually.

'Sure, I suppose.' Toby answered in a voice that would have said anything if it meant getting hot food.

'Ok. Let's shove them in the fire and see what happens.'

A few minutes later five charred nuggets were extracted from the glowing embers. Lots of blowing and flipping from hand-to-hand followed until the veggies were cool enough to be split open. Amazingly the insides were fluffy, steaming hot, and delicious.

'I never thought a burnt spud could be so tasty.' Toby, said chomping away like crazy.

'Or that straw could be so comfy,' said Sally, devouring her spud and piling straw around herself.

After eating, Sally gazed into the fiery embers. 'I've just thought of something really scary, Toby.'

'What. Besides being stuck in a time-travelling-nightmare, you mean?' said Toby, scraping mud from his shoes with a stick.

'I mean, what happens if we can't get ourselves out of this mess. Like, if we are stuck here forever in this-this horrible place. What happens then?'

Toby looked up from his shoes.

'Stuck here forever,' he said laughingly. 'Listen-up, Sal… because this is really important. We are *not* going to be stuck here forever, and we *will* be getting out of here. It's simply a matter of getting back to that machine and pressing the right buttons. That's all you need to keep in your head, Sally. Nothing else.'

'But what *if*, Toby. What *if?*'

Toby flashed a mischievous smile. 'Sally, you're not listening. We are going to get ourselves out of here, no matter how long it takes. That's just the way it's gonna be.'

'Really, Toby? You're not just trying to keep my spirits up?'

Toby leaned across and stared affectionately into Sally's worried eyes.

'I don't believe in spirits or ghosts. I believe in your intelligence and a teensy bit of my own intelligence.'

For the first time that day Sally allowed herself a little laugh.

'Thanks for that,' she said, wiping away a tear. 'And no matter what happens tomorrow, we mustn't run around like headless chickens again. We need to find the Thames and then Puddle Street.'

'Agreed,' said Toby. 'Headless chickens out, Thames in. I'm totally up for that. Right now though, my head is so scrambled I can hardly think straight. Tomorrow we'll need all our wits about us, so we really should try to get some sleep.'

Sally squashed down into the straw. 'Imagine waking-up tomorrow and finding this was all a bad dream.'

'Yeah, that would be something,' Toby agreed, as he snuggled down into the straw. 'But I wouldn't hold my breath on that happening.'

Less than a minute later Toby was amazed when he heard Sally snoozing her head off. Unfortunately he couldn't drift away quite so easily. His mind was still buzzing and on edge. The slightest sound made him twitch. Dogs barking in the distance, an owl hooting, voices carried on the wind, and from inside that nearby graveyard a spiky church tower staring down at him like a creepy stone giant.

Wiping his runny nose on his sleeve he continued watching and listening and doing his best to feel optimistic and positive. A few minutes later, with silvery moonlight pouring into the barn, he sucked in a wobbly breath, pulled his eyes shut, and slipped away into a deep uneasy sleep.

5. DON'T DROP THE BREAD!

Dawn at last. The sun shone brightly in a clear sky, and light rippled down through the broken rafters. Sally rubbed sleep from her eyes. They felt puffy, and her throat felt sore. She hauled herself into an upright position.

'So it wasn't just a bad dream, then!' she moaned, squinting at the sky and gazing around despairingly at the barn.

Raising her arms to stretch and yawn, she casually looked towards the ground. To her horror she discovered a posse of black rats enthusiastically nuzzling her toes. The rodents scattered in all directions when Sally started screaming like a loon.

'Wossup-wossup!' Toby cried, jumping unsteadily to his feet in a mad panic.

'Rats!' Sally squealed, curling her knees under her chin and pointing hysterically in no particular direction. 'Big hairy black things trying to eat my feet. I think I'm going to faint.'

Toby's empty belly rumbled so furiously he cared little about rats. Sally screamed again.

'Bloody hell, what's wrong now,' he grunted.

'Will you just look at this! I mean, LOOK!' Sally yelled. 'Never in my entire life has my hair been so filthy, so horrible. And.... oh-my-god, my back hurts even when I breathe.'

Toby's eyes widened.

'Well then, stop breathing,' he snapped.

'Hey Toby. Why are you being such a turd,' Sally

choked. 'My back really is hurting.'

'So! You're alive aren't you?' Toby snapped again. 'What more do you want?'

Sally's eyes came out on stalks. 'Did you just say *what more do I want?* Well, Einstein. I'll tell you what I want – how about you *getting me the hell out of here!!* Can you arrange that? No? I didn't think so. Instead, what about shutting your big fat stupid mouth.'

Toby had never seen Sally so angry. Not entirely sure how to react, he took a shaky breath. 'Jeez Sally. Let's try and calm down, yeah.'

'Well…you started it!' she glared, folding her arms.

Toby shook his head. 'I know. I'm sorry. It's just like… when I get this hungry I say the most stupid things.'

Sally wiped her eyes with her last tissue, folded it neatly, and then carefully shoved it up her sleeve.

'If that's the case you must be hungry all the time,' she sniffed, brushing down her jeans. 'And I still hate you.'

'I don't blame you.'

'Apology accepted though.'

'And you're right. I think I am hungry all the time. Which reminds me, before we start looking for rivers or streets, shouldn't we try and get a breakfast of some sort.'

'Oh Toby, I would *soooo* love that. But… any ideas how?'

'Not a sausage!'

'Please don't mention sausages… or toast… or scrambled eggs!'

'And I won't mention crispy bacon on the side, either.'

'Hardy har-har,' said Sally, shooting him a smirk.

'Let's see how funny you are a few hours from now.'

Exiting their little hideaway they unexpectedly found a bustling thoroughfare. Immediately the previous day's nightmare rolled straight back over them. It was different this time though: it was fifty times worse. In the cold light of a new day the milling crowds were even more milling and the scary feelings were even more scary. Along with the constant stink of open sewers, the reality of their situation came close to overwhelming them. Sally could only deal with the awful pong by stuffing bits of tissue up her nose.

'Yuck!' she coughed. 'We're definitely going to catch some weird bug from this.'

'At least our clothes don't stand out so much now,' said Toby, checking his filthy combats and Sally's even filthier jeans.

Toby was right. Except for an occasional glance at his not-so-spiky hair and Sally's nostril decorations, they mingled-in quite easily with the Saturday morning throngs. By that stage Toby was so maddeningly hungry he gawked longingly into the faces of anybody who even looked like they were eating something.

'Toby, will you stop doing that,' Sally demanded. 'I know you're hungry but its rude and it's attracting the wrong kind of attention.'

'Yeah, yeah, sure,' Toby nodded, before continuing with his gawking.

Without warning, Sally pulled the tissues from her nose and began sniffing the air like a hungry bloodhound. They both recognized it immediately; it was the indescribably gorgeous aroma of freshly baked bread. Like bees homing-in on a jam-jar they trailed after the smell.

'Look,' said Sally, nodding her head past Toby. 'It's

a bakery – a real live bakery!'

Sure enough, a chubby red-faced man covered in flour and sweat was busy piling hot steaming loaves onto a makeshift counter.

'Good morning, ladies,' he winked at the gaggle of shawl-covered women lined-up by the counter. 'I pray I haven't kept you waiting too long this fine morning?'

'This is torture,' Sally whimpered, enviously watching the women gather up the freshly baked loaves. 'I'm so hungry I could eat my own head... actually I could eat *your* head!'

'Yeah, and I'll be joining you,' Toby muttered, wistfully staring at the contents on the counter.

'Just think. All we've had to eat in two days is a disgusting turnip and a burnt potato.' Sally said grumpily.

'There's no need to remind me!' Toby said miserably.

'That's it... I've had enough,' Sally declared, with one hand on her hip and the her head turned sideways. 'My empty belly cannot be reasoned with. I think we need to... no-no, scratch that. I think *you* need to grab some of that bread. And don't look at me like that. I know what you're thinking, but I'm too hungry to debate rights-and-wrongs!'

'Hmmm...so when you say *grab* some bread – what you actually mean is *steal* some bread?'

'Toby, it is not stealing when starving to death is a possibility? It is simply procuring something to stay alive? And besides, you're such a fast runner no one would ever catch you. It'll be a cinch, ok... so chop-chop, let's go!' She commanded, backing-up her orders with a hefty shove. 'I'll be down the road a bit while you get on with it.'

Almost as an afterthought she added. 'Come to think of it, two loaves mightn't be a bad idea... or maybe three?

All right then, break a leg!'

'What! You want me to break someone's leg as well?'

'No silly. It's just an old theatre saying… means good luck, I think.'

'Okay, fine, whatever.'

While Toby scurried off to carry out his instructions, Sally sauntered down the street looking as inconspicuous as possible.

Two minutes later a chorus of yelling and shouting erupted from the direction of the bakery, followed by a mad-eyed Toby barrelling through the crowds with an irate posse on his heels.

'Stop thief!' a furious voice roared after him.

As Toby galloped past, Sally shouted. 'Don't… drop… the…bread! Whatever you do, don't…. drop….the bread!'

The dastardly bread thief sprinted away and quickly disappeared down a side street. All the exhausted posse could do was shout murderous obscenities after him.

Only when he felt out of danger did Toby stop running. A minute later, trotting along hurriedly, a smiling Sally joined him.

'Well done, my prince!' she said with a big smile. 'You handled that brilliantly. And if you weren't a common thief covered with manky sweat, I'd so give you a hug.'

'Thanks,' said Toby, his legs trembling like jelly. 'It's always nice to get positive feedback on your work.'

Like a pair of hungry vultures, they set about devouring their hard-won prize. Not long after – when they'd slacked a raging thirst in a nearby water trough, they sat back against a wall.

'Awrighty. Feeding time over,' Toby declared, chewing the last bit of crust. 'I was just thinking. It's very possible we spent most of yesterday going around in circles.'

'I agree. It did feel a bit like that.'

'And if that *was* the case, maybe Puddle Street wasn't so far away. In fact, when you think about it, it's probably only a mile or so from where we are right now. I'm guessing if we use our smarts – and use the river as a guide – with any luck we should be able to find it.'

'So long as I don't have to spend another night sleeping with rats, I'll do whatever you say.'

'First things first.' Toby continued, helping Sally to her feet. 'Let's go find the Thames.'

Half expecting another long and desperate search they could hardly believe their eyes when they rounded a bend and almost toppled into the river. And there it flowed, the good old Thames, minus all the 21st century bridges and embankments of course, but it was still the river they'd known all their lives.

'And will you look at those...' said Toby, gazing wide-eyed at scores of square-rigged ships, their masts jutting skywards like giant porcupine spines.

In fact Toby and Sally were slap bang in the middle of the city's mega-busy port area. 'Now *that's* what I call a sight to behold!' said Toby, bowled-over by the spectacle of tall ships, the packed wharfs, battalions of shouting dockers and huge wooden cranes creaking and groaning as they loaded and unloaded cargo.

'Yeah sure, it's cool to see, and all that,' said sally, anxious to get going again. 'But... Puddle Street?'

'Sure, of course, let's go!' said Toby, before running hotfoot past ships and cranes – checking and double-checking streets and backstreets all along the cramped slums spreading out towards the sea. All too soon the cold afternoon was beginning to creep towards another night. Fear and apprehension rushed over Sally.

'Maybe we could sneak aboard one of these ships, Toby. Just for tonight?' she suggested pleadingly. 'What do you think?'

'Uh-huh, maybe,' said Toby, trying to alleviate Sally's dread. 'But… that might not be as easy as it sounds.'

Just then, looming out of the mist and straddling the river like a great stretched-out house, a massive stone bridge began to emerge. Hundreds of people were busy criss-crossing along past rows and rows of painted houses and shops. Near the centre, where a tall watch turret stood, smoke poured out of a cluster of chimneys. swirling in slow motion over and beneath the huge archways of the mammoth structure.

'Crikey!' Sally said. 'I think that's old London Bridge. I recognise it from pictures in history class.'

'If that's what it *is* – brilliant!' Toby said eagerly. 'It's exactly for us.'

'What do you mean?'

'Follow me, and you'll see!'

Minutes later they were shoving their way through crowds of Londoners as they made their way towards the big granite northern entrance to the bridge.

'Oh gross… look at that, Sal,' said Toby sourly, staring horror-struck at a gruesome sight atop the entrance. 'I think they're human heads stuck on spikes – actual human heads!'

'Uggh… yes. I remember those from history class as well.'

'…but *actual* heads.'

'I know, Toby. They're horrible. But let's not make too big a deal about it. They were intended to warn off traitors and spies. And we do *not* need to look like either of those!'

'Okay then…' Toby said, urging Sally along. 'Let's get further along.'

As they inched their way along, the hum of easy-going chitter-chatter echoed along the cramped bridge. Near the middle section Toby hoisted himself onto the parapet of the guard wall. And with a hand over his eyes he gazed northwards across the river.

'Great! It's where I hoped it would be. It's the Tower of London, I'm sure of it.'

He was pointing towards a massive building with great ramparts and buttresses and huge flags waving tiredly in the breeze.

'Hey, just look at that,' Sally exclaimed, squinting across the river. 'It's definitely the Tower.'

'Which means…' said Toby, trailing a finger between the Tower and the westerly end of the old city. 'Puddle Street should be somewhere near…. *there!*'

'Toby, Toby!' Sally said quickly. 'I think I recognise that church. Don't you think it looks a bit like St. Paul's?'

Toby narrowed his eyes. 'Could very well be!' he said, nodding slowly. 'Let's get closer and check the area before it gets too dark.'

With great urgency they made their way back towards the entrance of the bridge. However, just as they rushed out through the entrance they were furiously howled out of the way by a dozen or so heavily armed horsemen thundering past in the direction of the Tower.

At the sight of mounted soldiers on horseback, Toby felt like a little boy again and just stood there, smiling stupidly from ear to ear. For some inexplicable reason, his grinning face caught the attention of a particularly tough looking soldier. Even as he galloped past he kept a malicious eye fixed on Toby.

For reasons Toby could never explain later, he casually raised a hand and waggled his fingers at the rider. It was just a silly little wave, but it was enough to bring the rider to a skidding halt.

'On no, what have you done?' Sally gasped in horror.

'Shit, shit, and double-shit!' Toby muttered. 'It was nothing – I only waved, honest!'

Quickly dismounting (along with two swarthy comrades) the rider marched back towards Toby and Sally. With arms as big as legs and a face that looked like it had been chopped-up and put back together in time for Halloween, he was the most ferocious looking man Toby had ever seen.

Toby could hardly breathe, and shrank under the glare of the approaching soldier. At the last second he instinctively pushed Sally into the crowd. The other riders, by that stage, were also pulling up. The Commanding Officer was not at all happy with the hold up.

'What in the King's name is going on back there?' he bellowed.

'This one here, Captain Pepper sir,' the ferocious rider barked, hauling Toby up by his collar like a noose. 'He made an unruly gesture, he did. Splatt and Bilge will confirm that's what happened. Ain't that right lads?'

'Aye sir, he made an unruly gesture,' replied a goblin-like corporal. 'And we wants to know why?'

With blazing eyes, the soldier frog-marched Toby by the scruff of the neck, back towards the captain. As soon as the captain heard what the so-called "unruly gesture" was, he shook his head in consternation.

'Sergeant Bloodnutt, the only reason I don't have you horsewhipped twice a day is because, most of the time, you are a damn fine Tower guard. But by the sword of

Jupiter, my patience is fast running out. Release that boy immediately and get back to your horse.'

'Sir, I ---?'

'...get back to your horse *now,* soldier!'

Meanwhile, a throng of spectators had assembled hoping for a free blood-letting display between a mad soldier and an idiot kid. Following the captain's intervention they booed and laughed at the big sergeant: his angry face now tightening like a mangled sausage. No matter what the captain said, his wounded pride demanded action. And sure enough just as he turned to leave, a deadly knife sliced through the air.

'Oooooooooohhh...' the watching crowd buzzed approvingly. A knife! This was much more like it.

One wrong move and Toby knew he was toast. And so, to avoid being chopped in two, he spun around and karate-kicked the sergeant as hard as possible in the centre of his chest. Such a kick would have knocked a mule over. But amazingly the sergeant barely stirred. Instead, with lightning speed, he swiped the blade again, this time missing Toby's nose by half a millimetre.

'Aaaaaaaaaaahhh...' the crowd buzzed again, delighted with the unfolding action. No doubt the idiot kid would be slaughtered as soon as the sergeant finished teasing out the situation.

But before the show reached a blood-spattered climax the voice of the captain rang out once more.

'Bloodnutt, I will not tell you again, get back to your horse.'

The mad sergeant's aggression was too much for Toby. Taking his chance, he abruptly turned tail and dived headlong through the wall of spectators.

'Meet me at the chopped heads!' he shouted back in Sally's general direction, before he disappeared out of sight.

A caterwaul of booing and jeering followed the sergeant and his swarthy sidekicks as they slouched back to their mounts.

'Mark my words. Someday I will make that runt pay for this.' Bloodnutt cursed under his breath.

Going by this latest terrifying incident Sally was convinced that half the population of London was out to get them. And when she didn't immediately find Toby among the crowds passing under the chopped heads, a wave of panic ballooned inside her heart.

"Toby, Toby, Where have you *got* to?" she whispered worriedly.

A tap on the shoulder made her jump.

'What kept you, Bunn?' Toby's smiling face asked as he popped up behind her.

Sally whacked him around the ears. 'Don't you *dare* leave me like that again,' she snapped. 'I thought you were dead!'

'Hey Sal, I didn't mean to scare you.' Toby explained with an uneasy laugh. 'I was just making sure that nut-job Tower guard was well and truly gone.'

Sally ran a hand through her hair. 'I know you didn't mean it, Toby. It was just such a horrible feeling being suddenly here on my own.'

'I felt exactly the same. But... I think I may have found something that will cheer you right up. Take a peek over here.'

Toby gestured towards a great mish-mash of buildings sprawled out in front of them. Sally stared hard.

'Ok then, what exactly am I looking for?'

'Just up there... on that rise.' Toby pointed. 'Doesn't that building look like the old Alms House? You know, the one behind Puddle Street. It was a soup kitchen for a while last winter, remember?'

Sally followed the line of Toby's finger across the maze of buildings. 'I guess…maybe…' she replied doubtfully. 'But doesn't the old Alms House have a clock tower?'

'It does. But it's the main building you need to concentrate on. I'm guessing the clock section was added much later.'

Concentrating hard, Sally's eyes narrowed as tight as they could.

'Hey…yes!' she said delightedly. 'I-I see what you mean. I never would have noticed that.' And immediately they set off in what they hoped would be the final leg of their journey.

It was already early evening when they reached the vicinity of the Alms house. Toby's eyes lit up.

'Sally, I definitely know this road?'

'Yes, it does look familiar.' Sally eagerly agreed.

'It's more than just familiar. It's going in the same bendy direction as the lane running up from the southern end of the street. I think we're almost there.'

In the middle of deciding what direction they should take next, they suddenly found themselves looking down Puddle Street. After all the calamities and the mad encounters with yobs and psycho killers, they had made it back in one piece.

'I can hardly believe it.' Toby said quietly, holding onto Sally's trembling hand. 'There it is…. right in front of us.'

Taking a deep breath to steady their nerves, and with a freezing night gathering around them, they once again walked along lovely old Puddle Street.

6. HOME SWEET HOME

'Toby, do *not* forget. We need to look like butter wouldn't melt in our mouths. We're just a couple of kids from up-north who got ourselves lost in the big city, ok?'

Toby nodded. 'You betcha, and then we throw ourselves at his mercy.'

'Too right we throw ourselves at his mercy. And remember… I do the talking. And also, no matter what happens, do not lose your cool or get angry. You'll be *so* totally dead if you do.'

With her hands balled into fists, Sally resolutely climbed the steps of No 2. 'Fingers crossed!' She whispered back at Toby.

And then, finally, gulping down a big nervous breath, she banged the shiny brass knocker three times.

Seconds crawled into a lingering minute.

She was about to knock again when a clinking and clanking of locks and bolts jangled from inside. The door creaked open just wide enough for a little nose to peek out.

'You two were here yesterday,' a voice said.

'That's right, sir. We were indeed here yesterday.' Sally cooed in her sweetest little girl voice. 'And what happened was a stupid misunderstanding and entirely our fault.'

'Aye… it was your fault. But what's that got to do with me?' The voice asked, though not unkindly.

'Well actually, we were wondering if we might take a minute of your time to explain things?'

'Don't need explaining. You just need to push off.'

In actual fact, the little scruff was hugely surprised to see the two strangers back again. He was even more surprised at how cold, filthy and frightened they looked.

'Listen mate,' Toby blurted, ignoring the pact about who was to do the talking. 'We're in big trouble, yeah. You see the thing is, we came down from *up north* to look for a better life in London. And well… we got ourselves seriously lost and in trouble. I know it's asking a lot, but we were hoping you might let us stay here for a bit. Just till we get things sorted with work and the like. And of course we'll earn our keep, clean the house – stuff like that, or whatever else you need doing. So please mate, do you think you can help us?'

'…and I swear we won't cause you a minute's bother,' exclaimed Sally, finally getting a word in edgeways.

For a second or two the little nose didn't move. Then a big brown eye peeped out to give them a proper once over. A moment later the door swung open. Sally almost swooned with relief. Their whopper of a lie seemed to be working.

'And where did you stay last night?' the scruff asked, his resolve wilting. 'Surely not out in all that rain?'

Toby seized on the scruff's curiosity. 'We had no choice, mate. It was pretty awful being outdoors last night I can tell you. Isn't that right, Sally---?'

Sally was busy taking a proper look at their potential rescuer. He really was quite scruffy. On the plus side though, he had a kind face and friendly brown eyes that sparkled with warmth and curiosity.

Toby nudged Sally. 'I said, *isn't that right,* Sally?'

'Y-Yes it is,' Sally answered falteringly, struggling to play her part as convincingly as Toby. 'And to be honest I don't think I can face it again.'

'And eh, there is something I really need to know about yesterday,' the scruff began in a low voice. And although Toby suspected what the question might be, he nearly lost his nerve when the scruff leaned in closer.

'How did you get in here? Was it when I were at work? Did I leave a window open or what?'

'Yeah, yeah, that was it... that window there... you left it open just wide enough.'

'Aye, I guessed as much. I've gotten a bit lazy when it comes to checking the windows. And you probably thought the place was empty since it was all so new looking.'

'You took the words right out of my mouth,' said Toby, almost passing out with relief. 'To be honest we were kinda desperate and needed somewhere to kip for the night. And as for all that *uncle* stuff, I was talking rubbish, mainly out of fear of that poker you were waving about.'

Nodding his acceptance of Toby's explanation, the scruff smiled. 'And I have to admit I were just as scared as you. But I reckoned the poker would do the trick.'

A flicker of firelight in the background only made Toby more determined to get back inside. And so, forgetting his promises to Sally, he readied himself to charge the door if it started to close again. But he needn't have worried. The scruff was well and truly convinced.

'Well, you better come in then,' he offered, ushering them indoors. 'We can't stand out here jabbering all evening.'

Toby and Sally could hardly believe it. They were back in the hallway of No 2 Puddle Street staring longingly towards the upstairs landing. At that point Toby realised Sally had been spot-on. Any wrong moves would prove disastrous. They must play-out this situation very coolly.

Secretly, the scruff was rather pleased at the prospect of two exotic out-of-towners staying with him. He saw hundreds of young strangers arriving in London every day. So nobody knew better what it was like to be friendless and hungry in the big city. He was an inquisitive chap by nature, and even as he led them into the sitting room he couldn't help staring at Toby

'Your hair,' he said, curiosity getting the better of him.

'What.... what about my hair?' Toby asked, feeling his head.

''Tis all pointy and such. You look like you seen a ghost.'

Feeling a tad peeved, Toby stared hard at the scruff. He was right of course. In the last twenty-four hours his normally well-groomed mane had become a nest for all kinds of grubby substances.

'Ah well, you know how it is,' Toby shrugged helplessly. 'Sleeping rough and whatnot. It's no wonder my hair is, as you say, all pointy and such.'

'Well lucky for you I knows a fine barber.' The scruff said, slapping Toby on the shoulder. 'So don't you worry none, we'll get that mess sorted out in no time.'

Sally sensed it was time to change the subject.

'I was thinking we should probably introduce ourselves,' she said, forcing a smile. 'My name is Sally Bunn. And this is my... eh, cousin, Toby Sprocket.'

'Pleased to meet you both,' said the scruff, brightly. 'Inky Blyster is my name, and this is my uncle's new house. I'm looking after it for him, with my mother's help, while he's away on business. He'll be gone for a good while so there shouldn't be any problems with you staying for a bit.'

Toby and Sally stared at each other.

Inky Blyster! Why... that was one of the names in the cubbyhole!

'P-Pleased to meet you, Inky Blyster.' Sally stuttered, all at once pale and shaky.

'Likewise,' said an equally dazed Toby, clasping Inky's hand and giving it a firm shake.

Won over entirely by his new chums, Inky believed it was only good manners to converse freely.

'Aye, me too – pleased to meet you. And if you think it was cold yesterday you should have been here last month,' he began, while showing his guests into the room with the fireplace.

'Sit, please. Now where was I? Oh yes, the Thames freezing over. Hard as a rock it was. There was skating and sliding and all sorts of fun. And boy did I have the best time ever with my friend Herbert Herring. Which reminds me... tomorrow is Sunday, so Herbert will be over for breakfast. You'll like Herbert. Everyone likes Herbert. And my mother will also be here: she cooks a great breakfast on a Sunday, does my mother.'

Again Sally and Toby stared in disbelief.

'Sorry Inky. Did you say, Herbert Herring?' Sally asked.

'Yes I did. We both work in the Globe theatre across the river. That's the theatre you know.... Do you have actors and plays up north?'

'Oh yes. Lots.' Sally replied, still reeling at the Blyster-Herring revelations.

'Aye, the good old Globe. We have great times there, Herbert and me. We used to work there with another best friend, Sid Dripping. But he's gone very strange since he's taken up with that swine Christian *blasted* Hemlock.'

That was the first time Toby and Sally heard the name of Christian Hemlock. And the way the name left Inky's mouth was like pure poison.

'And what exactly happened to him… this Sid chap?' Sally enquired.

With sadness etched on his face, Inky sat back in his chair and drummed his fingers on the armrest.

'You'll hardly believe this, but up to a couple of weeks ago, the three of us did everything together. And I do mean everything. Like brothers we were. In fact, Sid spent more nights sleeping on that couch than he ever did over at his own place. Long story short he just turned his back on all his friends and went to work for that murdering gangster, Hemlock.'

For a short while an awkward silence filled the room.

Inky sighed deeply. 'Like I said, everyone likes Herbert. My mother can be a bit serious sometimes. But she's a saint really, my mother. You'll see, tomorrow.'

He then raised a finger. 'Oh, I've just thought of something really interesting.'

'And what's that, Inky?' Toby asked tentatively, fearing bad news might be on the way.

'You'll be needing work, right? Well, there's a brand-new play starting over at the Globe soon, and that means there'll be jobs going…. not for you, Sally, 'cos you're just a girl. But if you get in there, Toby, I don't see any problems. The job might only be temporary, and the pay isn't great, but it it's not a bad place to work.'

Because of her yearning to get to the machine, Sally ignored the *just-a-girl* slur and remained doe-eyed and smiley. But the evening was getting along and Inky was still chatting like he'd never run out of steam.

It was time to act.

Sally rubbed her eyes and yawned loudly. Reading

the signals Toby added his own shouty yawn.

'Lordy, what am I thinking of?' Inky exclaimed apologetically. 'I'm sure all you want is sleep. And there's me rabbiting on. Thing is though,' he added. 'All the spare bedrooms are full of builder's junk. Which means the only place fit for sleeping in is the attic. And I hope you won't mind, but my uncle has an ugly looking contraption stored there?'

'No,no,no, we don't mind at all,' Sally said smiling. 'It sounds blissful compared to last night. And as a matter of fact we love contraptions. Don't we, Toby?'

'Oh yeah. Can't get enough of them. We could look at contraptions all day. So don't concern yourself, Inky. We're just happy to have a safe place to sleep.'

'Good, that's settled then,' said Inky said, rubbing his hands together. 'I'll go grab some bedding.'

With sidelong glances at each other, Toby and Sally followed Inky up the stairs towards the attic.

'Here we are,' Inky announced, pushing the attic door open. 'Your new sleeping quarters.'

And there it was. The Mark 5. It looked safe and sound under an old blanket just waiting to take them home. Sally was close to bursting into tears. Inky, meanwhile, was busy organizing a pair of straw mattresses beside the machine. He also fixed a candle on the floor, its flickering light lending a nice homely feel.

'It's a bit chilly, I know. But we'll get a fire going tomorrow and heat the place up. Righto then, I'll be saying goodnight and we'll have a proper talk about the Globe in the morning.'

Right at that moment, Toby and Sally didn't care a jot about the Globe, or chilly attics, or anything else. They were moments away from going home and all they felt was gratitude for their unwitting saviour. Sally looked at

Inky with something like awe.

'My dear Inky Blyster,' she said, struggling to hold back the tears. 'You're an amazing guy. And you will never know how much this means to us. I can only wish you good luck with the rest of your life.'

'Yeah, same here, pal,' said Toby, with another firm shake of the hand. 'We couldn't have done it without you.'

Taken aback by this sudden seriousness, and not at all sure what it was they couldn't have done without him, Inky looked befuddled.

'Huh... well... eh...don't mention it,' he shrugged. ''Tis only a straw mattress. You'd do the same for me I'm sure.'

'Of course we would,' said Sally. 'We would do everything possible for a chap like you.'

Awkwardly backing his way out of the attic, Inky muttered 'goodnight' a bunch more times before eventually pulling the door closed.

*

For a long careful minute Toby and Sally listened as Inky's footsteps tramped all the way down the stairs. Finally, with great sighs of relief, they were alone with the professor's machine.

'I know this might sound strange,' Sally whispered. 'But I felt guilty for not telling him the truth.'

'I know, me too. But most likely he'd have thrown us straight out again if we did.'

When they rolled back the blanket from the machine, a bright new moon shone down through the attic window, drenching the Mark 5 in a silvery glow.

'I don't know about you, Toby. But the last 24 hours

felt like a mad-wide-awake dream.'

'A wide-awake nightmare, you mean,' Toby said quickly, pushing the blanket to the floor. 'Either way it's time to put an end to it.'

'I'll second that,' Sally beamed. 'Let's get going!'

The canopy hadn't been fully closed so it didn't make a sound when Toby pulled it open. Being especially careful then, so as not to touch any of the controls, they lowered themselves down into the cockpit before silently locking the canopy into position.

'I think you should do the honours,' said Sally, nodding towards the control panel.

With his heart hammering, Toby held a trembling finger over the big red switch.

'Go on, Toby. Just do it!'

'Phew. Ok then. Here goes.'

Taking a deep breath, Toby lowered his finger and flicked the switch.

Pushing themselves back into the seats... they waited... and waited... and then waited some more....!

Apart from the faintest rumble in the bowels of the machine, nothing had changed. Nothing. Not another sound was heard.

'Please-oh-please, don't let this be happening!' Sally cried, a haunted look spreading on her face.

'Why don't you try it, Sal.' Toby said softly. 'Maybe I'm doing something wrong?'

'Yeah, yeah, of course. That could be it,' Sally agreed, nodding nervously. 'Here goes nothing again.'

Agonizingly, no matter how often she flicked, pulled, or pressed the big red switch, along with every other switch on the control panel, the Mark 5 remained obstinately silent. Their dream of going home had been cruelly snatched away from their grasp. All of a sudden it felt like the house and the attic and even the sky was crushing down on them.

'It's broken... the damned thing is broken!' Toby exploded, thumping the panel in frustration.

'Stopit-stopit...' Sally cried, her voice clear and cold. 'Smashing it to pieces won't help the situation.'

'It never entered my head it might not work,' said Toby, trying to compose himself. 'I just can't believe it.'

'Me neither,' said Sally, helplessly. 'But could it be we're not doing it right... or maybe it's something we're forgetting? What was it the professor said about ignition procedures and stuff like that?'

Toby racked his brain.

'Oh I don't know. I mean with all that was happening, I hardly remember a word.'

The awfulness and the utter disappointment was too much for Sally. Holding her face she began crying in great sobs. Toby put his arm around her shoulder and lulled her into his chest.

'Sally. None of this is easy, I know. But we will sort something out, you'll see.'

Sally raised head back and sucked a giant breath into her lungs. 'Ok then. Enough of that,' she said determinedly, wiping her tear-smudged eyes and sniffly nose with the back of her hand.

'Feeling sorry for ourselves won't solve a thing. We need to find out what's wrong with the machine and try to fix it. Obviously we can't start banging and hammering at this late hour. So we should just try to sleep and decide what's best to do in the morning.'

As he spread blankets across the straw mattresses, Toby finished her thoughts. 'And seeing we've already survived been attacked by soldiers, chased by madmen, not to mention nearly starving to death. Fixing a time machine should be easy-peasy.'

'That's exactly the spirit we need,' said Sally, clambering out of the machine. 'We have to stay positive.'

Snuggling down then into their comfy quilts, a pitter-pitter of raindrops began dancing across the roof.

'At least we're not outside in that.' Sally said with a shiver.

'Boy, you can say that again.'

Sally pulled the big wooly blanket over her head, chewed her lip and yawned for a full minute.

'I suppose we should at least try to get some sleep.'

'Yeah, of course. Night then, Sal. See you in the morning.'

Toby began squirming and shifting before lying on his back and staring at nothing.

'Sally…'

'What, Toby…'

'Guess what I'm thinking?'

'Eh… never again will you sit in a machine your uncle built,' Sally said drolly.

'No – although that *is* a good answer. No…I was thinking. Those jobs over at the Globe. Not such a crazy idea now, huh?'

'No. Not crazy at all.'

'Isn't it weird we're actually thinking that, never mind saying it!'

'It sure is….' said Sally, her mouth commencing another giant yawn. 'And since I'm on the verge of passing out. Could you stop talking now, please.'

'No probs…' said Toby, leaning over and blowing the candle out.

As he lay there listening to the rain, Toby reached up to wipe the steamed-up attic window. As his fingers made a squeaking sound along the watery surface, he thought about all the stuff in his old bedroom – the football posters, his new TV, those model aeroplanes he'd made as a small kid, and all the other ordinary things he had taken so much for granted. They were like beacons of hope in a world gone completely bonkers. And just then, likely because for the first time in two days he wasn't screaming and running in blind terror, he noticed his heart was beating normally. Closing his eyes, he smiled. And before he realized it was happening, he joined Sally in a desperately needed snore.

7. MRS. BLYSTER DECIDES

Next morning arrived bright, clear, and frosty, and although the attic was cold as a fridge, Toby and Sally were already in the machine pulling and pushing every switch, button and lever. But it was all to no avail. Nothing miraculous had happened during the night. The Mark 5 was as dead as a doorknob.

'You know what I'm thinking,' Toby said, tapping his chin. 'I'm thinking electric power is what's missing. I mean, all the instruments look like they're working fine: it's just, nothing is registering on the power grid gauge. Which doesn't make sense since there are two huge batteries under the seats – here, look…' Toby lifted a seat and pointed.

'So what are you saying?' Sally asked, folding her arms in frustration. 'That we're stuck here forever… that-that we could be starting a life sentence?'

'No, of course not. I'm just saying more-then-likely something really simple is causing the problem: like say a minor electrical fault or maybe something as basic as a loose wire.'

'It had better be that simple or this pile of junk is for the scrapheap!' Sally declared, jabbing an accusatory thumb at the machine and kicking at it as she passed.

To her horror, the kick flipped-open a small door at the back of the machine.

'Oh no-no-no….' she whimpered. 'I hardly touched it, Toby. I swear.'

To their great relief, instead of releasing a new calamity, a tatty notebook and a tiny toolbox tumbled out of a small compartment. Grabbing them up, Toby began skimming through the notebook. His mouth fell open in astonishment.

'Why, this is fantastic!'

'What! What's fantastic?'

Turning page after page, Toby's eyes shone with excitement.

'It's uncle Arthur's notebook, and its full of technical notes and drawings... *loads* of drawings. Every little detail about the machine as it was actually being constructed. It's all here, check it out.'

Leaning in, Sally gazed at the notebook. 'And its useful to us how?'

'Well, now should be able to take the engine apart, find where the problem is, fix it, and reassemble everything.'

A crooked smile spread across Sally's face.

'Yeaaaah, that's brilliant. But before we start pulling things apart. What happens if Inky finds engine parts scattered around the attic? Or his mum? Or his friend Herbert? Worse still, what if they remove something vital... even by accident. What happens then?'

Toby squeezed his face. 'You're right. Never thought of that. Could be a disaster waiting to happen.'

'And I don't think we need that!'

Toby thought hard.

'Ok then. What about this. After we remove a component for checking and cleaning, we put it straight back in when we're finished. That way no one will be suspicious, parts won't be misplaced, *and* we'll be less likely to make a mistake. It might take us a bit longer, but it will be safer.'

'Genius idea!' said Sally, followed by a high-five. 'For the moment, though, shouldn't we hide the notebook and the toolbox under the seats *and* lock the canopy shut, just in case.'

'Genius idea number two!' Toby nodded, followed by another high-five.

They were so busy congratulating each other they never heard someone coming up the stairs. A rap-rap on the door made them jump. It was Inky, entering slowly with a pitcher of warm water and some linen cloths.

'Rise-n-shine lazybones,' he called out merrily. 'Its eight o'clock already.'

With just seconds to spare, Sally managed to throw the notebook and the toolbox under the seat, lock down cockpit, and pull the blanket over the machine.

'Heeeey... Inky... good morning!' She announced chirpily, leaning casually on the machine.

'And good morning to you, Miss Sally... and to you, Master Toby. I hope you both slept well. Herbert and my mother are downstairs cooking-up some eggs and toast. I should warn you though, my mother is especially anxious to meet you *and* give you a grilling.'

'Eggs and toast?' said Toby, deaf to everything after the mention of food. 'Like... *real* eggs and toast?'

'Yes... *real* eggs and toast. What other kinds are there? Anyhow, you better hurry along before Herbert scoffs the lot.'

As soon as they had washed and scrubbed, Toby and Sally hurried downstairs, before rather self-consciously, entering the kitchen. There they were met by the most wonderfully delicious mouth-watering smell in the world – chunks of bread toasted in front of the fire and slathered in salty butter. It was all they could do not to pass-out with craving.

Herbert Herring, meanwhile, was chatting away to a smiling Mrs. Annie Blyster who in turn was busy arranging stacks of hard-boiled eggs and piles of buttered toast across the long kitchen table. Small and plump as a kettle, Mrs. Blyster had a mop of curly brown hair and two piercing blue eyes that could see through waffle from twenty paces.

'Good morning, Mrs. Blyster and... Mr. Herring, I presume?' Sally said, demurely arching her eyebrows. 'I am so very pleased to meet you both.'

Tall and lean with thick brown hair, Herbert Herring had bright inquisitive blue eyes and a sharp intelligent face. And just like Inky's mother, he too was on high alert especially when it came to newcomers who appeared out of nowhere.

Straight off the bat Mrs. Blyster got down to business. 'I'm sure you are very pleased,' she scowled, wiping her hands on her apron while closely scrutinising this Sally person. 'But before you get *too* pleased with yourself, I want to talk about a dim-witted London lad who gives away free board and lodgings to strangers and interlopers.'

'I told you, Mother' said a scarlet-faced Inky. 'Tis only till they get sorted.'

'...*and* he's normally such a sensible boy. Never gets into trouble or hangs around street corners – not like some of the upstarts I know around here. And look how clean he is.'

'Mother pleeeease----'

'Inky!' Mrs. Blyster said loudly raising her index finger. Inky instantly fell silent.

Mrs. Blyster resumed her inspection of the interlopers and Toby flashed one of his best stellar smiles in her direction.

'Mrs. Blyster. I would just like to say---'

'...Yes, I imagine you would like to say *lots* of

things,' Mrs. Blyster cut across Toby. 'But frankly my lad, you can save your blather for somebody who gives a hoot. I'm here to make sure a pair of fly-by-nights aren't also a pair of hoodwinkers.'

Before Toby could say another word, Mrs. Blyster had plonked herself in front Toby, knotted her brow into a tangle of concentration, and gazed penetratingly into his startled eyes. First right-to-left, then left-to-right, then back to right-to-left.

'Hm hmmmmmmm,' she murmured, mentally processing the information she seemed to have garnered from Toby's eyeballs.

'Tis enough for now. Step aside. And now you, my girl.' she declared, clicking her fingers in Sally's direction. 'Over here!'

Sally dutifully took-up her position.

'Uh-huuuuuuh,' Mrs. Blyster murmured again, raising her left eyebrow and giving Sally an equally penetrating examination.

'The eyes never lie,' she declared. 'They are the windows to the soul. And therefore I can truthfully say we have two honest souls here. So yes, you may stay. But only for a trial period, mind. And remember… we're not running a doss house here. You pay your way or it's out the door. In other words, get a job. There will be no backsliding or dillydallying. Are we clear on that?'

'Of course, Mrs. Blyster,' Sally replied, smilingly. 'We are both very clear on that.'

'Good, excellent…,' Mrs. Blyster said, even though her left eyebrow remained sceptically raised.

Gathering-up her kettles and pans and bits and bobs, she kissed her son on his reddening cheek. 'I'm a busy woman and can't be lazing around here all day. So I'll say good morning to you all.'

'Thanks for everything, Mother,' Inky said, his cheeks aflame. 'And you won't forget the mutton stew for later.'

'Of course not. And I'll make sure there's enough for four hungry mouths.' She then pointed at the newcomers. 'And remember you two, no backsliding. Get a job or its out the door you'll be.' And with that Mrs. Blyster scampered out the front door like a chubby whirlwind.

Toby hurriedly introduced himself to Herbert.

'Hi, I'm Toby, this is Sally, and excuse my manners, but I so need to start eating.'

'Tuck right in!' said Herbert, motioning towards the breakfast goodies. 'And I'm pleased to meet you both.'

In thirty seconds flat Toby had demolished five hard-boiled duck eggs, four doorstep slices of buttery toast and at least a pint and a half of goats' milk. Sally wasn't far behind with four boiled eggs, two doorstep slices of toast, and maybe a half pint of milk.

'Dynamite.' Toby declared, while chewing and belching and wiping his mouth with his forearm. 'Absolute dynamite.'

'I must say,' Herbert said admiringly. 'That's one helluva way to gobble down a breakfast.'

*

It was at that very first breakfast that Toby discovered how much the Inky and Herbert loved hearing stories. For as soon as he began filling their ears with tales of his derring-dos' and heroic deeds, the two boys were in the palm of his hand. They had never heard of such bravery. Neither had Sally, and she'd been right there with him.

'Gosh!' Herbert gasped admiringly. 'You fought off Dungworth and his thugs, and *then* kicked a seven feet tall trooper straight into his chest… in front of everybody. Wow!'

'Wowser for me too….' Sally beamed, her eyes widening. 'A seven-foot tall trooper. And tell us, Toby. Was he like the "Thing" in Fantastic Four? A-A-And when you kicked him did ear-wax shot out of his ears? Huh did it, Toby, did it?'

Ignoring Sally, Toby continued. 'I had no choice, Herbert. Sometimes bravery can be a curse. It was either him or me, and of course I had to protect Sally.'

'Goes without saying.' Inky agreed, nodding slowly.

'And weren't you lucky to have Toby around?' Herbert said to Sally.

'Oh yes indeedy,' Sally replied tersely. 'Lucky is one word that can describe Super-Toby. There are also other words though, words like---'

'…whoa there now, Sal,' Toby light-heartedly cut in. 'I'm sure the guys don't want to hear about us all day. Also, Inky. You mentioned last night about jobs at the Globe?'

'Aye, that's right. There's a new play coming-up. And old Burbage is interviewing this very day for extra workers. In fact, if you're up for it, and we go out right now to check it. He can be a bit of a grump Burbage, but mostly he is easy to get on with. I don't think you'll have any problems.'

'That's good to hear!' Sally said eagerly. 'But like, is there stuff we should know first. Like what to say and what *not* to say? You know the kind of thing.'

Inky and Herbert looked awkwardly at each other. 'No offense intended, Miss Sally.' Herbert quietly explained. 'But… you're a girl.'

'You don't say? Moi! A girl?' Sally said jokingly. 'And there was me thinking I was a monkey with a nice hairdo.'

'I-I-I just thought---'

'...fiddlesticks, Herbert. We need jobs...*both* of us need jobs. You heard what Mrs. Blyster said. We have to start paying our way or we're out on our ears.'

'I know all that, Sally. But the problem is – girls have never work at the Globe, *ever!*'

'So what? Can't we at least give it a try,' said Sally. 'It won't hurt just to give it a try, will it?'

'Well, no, I suppose not, since you put it that way.' Herbert conceded. 'We just don't want to see you disappointed, you know – if things don't go well.'

Sally smiled confidently. 'My mum always said, "you never know what's round the next corner till you go round the next corner."'

Giving a one-shoulder shrug, Inky turned to Herbert. 'Why not?'

'Ok then,' Herbert smiled. 'Lets go!'

8. THE BIG INTERVIEW

Not long after that fateful Sunday morning in the Winter of 1610 the four new friends swung out across London Bridge. A bitter wind whined like a hungry dog as it cut through the cold morning air. It didn't bother Toby and Sally in the least: they felt peculiarly uplifted as they tromped along roads streaked with muck and frost. They wondered about this new adventure they were embarking upon. Would it be too dangerous? Would it be too difficult? To distract herself from such worries, Sally tried to picture this part of London, her London, in the early 21st century. She was surprised to discover how little she clearly remembered.

'By the way,' said Inky, interrupting her thoughts. 'I was thinking about what you asked earlier, Sally. And there are a couple of things that might help with old Burbage.'

'Great, Inky. Such as?'

'First – always look him straight in the eye, and second – always call him *Mister* or *Sir* or maybe both. You see, he's a big boss and likes to be shown proper respect'

'That's right,' Herbert nodded. 'Playing the old *Sir* and *Mister* cards… always works, and always keeps you in the good books.'

'Thanks guys, much appreciated,' said Sally, her voice bright and firm.

Lots of traipsing and walking followed, until they finally reached the north end of Tooley Street and the home of Mr. Burbage. Even at that early hour the street was filled with children playing, adults shouting and a constant flow of chatter spilling out of windows and doors.

'It's just along here on the corner,' said Herbert, gesturing down the street.

Like so many of the houses in the old city, Burbage's place was a big old ramshackle building that looked slightly lopsided and bulged out in the middle like a brick belly.

'Oh no!' Herbert moaned, spotting a bunch of young men already lined-up outside the house. 'This is not a good sign.'

It turned out that Herbert needn't have worried. Most of the applicants were being shuffled in-and-out in double-quick time. And no sooner had the pals reached the open front door, than a gravelly voice bellowed 'Next!'

Moments later Toby and Sally were standing in a small poorly-lit room stuffed with the smells of tobacco, damp and mothballs. On one side of the room a heavy velvet curtain was draped across a bay window while on the opposite wall were old posters of Globe productions and a big faded map of England. A huge desk, strewn with documents and papers and two fat candles that smoked like chimneys, filled the back of the room. Installed between the candles sat the imposing figure of Mr. Richard Burbage clad in a fancy embroidered dressing gown and scribbling earnestly with a long feathery quill.

'Name… age… address?' he said tiredly, his attention staying fixed on his paperwork.

'Toby Sprocket…twelve…Puddle Street. *sir*.'

'Sally Bunn…twelve…Puddle Street. *Sir*. We're cousins you see.'

73

As soon as the word 'Sally' entered his eardrums, Burbage fixed a monocle to his left eye and scowled between the flaming candles.

'Egad!' he cried, his hands gripping the armrests, 'You're a girl!'

'Quite correct, Mister Burbage, *sir.*' Sally replied graciously. 'I am definitely a member of the female gender.'

As if sucking an especially sucky sweet, Burbage puckered his mouth as he surveyed the two teenagers.

'I venture you do not hail from our wondrous city.'

'That is correct, sir.' Sally confirmed. 'We are from up north and keen to find work in your wonderful city.'

'Hmmmm indeed,' Burbage mumbled, making a steeple with his fingers and giving Toby a close inspection. Compared to those he had just dismissed, Toby looked full of health and vigour.

'Congratulations, Master Sprocket. You are hired. First thing tomorrow morning you will report to Mr. Mullion in the props department. He will discuss your duties and show you the ropes.'

Toby was over the moon. 'Thank you, Mr. Burbage, sir. You won't regret hiring me. I promise you that, sir.'

'I had better not, lad. I take a dim view of time wasters. You'll be out that door quicker than you can say Jack Spratt if you are one of those.'

Tut-tutting and stroking his chin, Burbage turned his monocled eye towards an increasingly nervous Sally.

'And what do you do, my child?' he asked, rather loudly, in case Sally was slightly deaf. 'Sweeping, cleaning, that kind of thing... yes?'

'Sweeping, cleaning, that kind of thing... noooo.... not my scene, Mr. Burbage. However, I am rather good at history, *very* good at English, and *brilliantly* good at mathematics.'

Steepling his fingers again, Burbage crossed his ankles and sat back into his chair.

'Is that so,' he smiled, removing his monocle. 'The education system up north seems to have improved immeasurably since my last visit. Unfortunately, while you may well be excellent at all of those subjects: you are still a member of the female gender. And it is sturdy boys we require here. So I am afraid---'

'...Mr. Burbage,' Sally cut in. 'Ask me any mathematical question and I will answer it correctly.'

As it happened Burbage had a list of awkward business figures laid out in front of him. And before Sally could take another breath, he shot a question at her.

'73 multiplied by 5, minus 127, divided by 2?'

'119!' Sally answered in a flash.

Burbage nearly slid off the end of his quill. 'I-I say, that is correct.'

Sitting to attention then, Burbage reeled-off a string of especially difficult mathematical questions. But no matter what he fired at Sally in whatever arrangement, she folded her arms and calmly fired back the correct answers. Needless to say, Burbage was mightily impressed. Luckily for Sally, what Burbage couldn't see was her phone calculator cradled in her arms *and* her finely tuned texting-thumb tapping away like crazy. And he certainly couldn't know that Sally's accountant father had taught her the basics of bookkeeping – which she excelled at. For a few seconds Burbage studied Sally's face, searching for some kind of clue that her skill was all part of a sneaky trick. Deep down though he knew it wasn't a trick – he was completely won over.

'Never did I think I would ever be uttering these words... but, congratulations *Miss* Sally Bunn, you are hired. Mind you, it's a trial period only. Should you pass, however, the job will be yours permanently. So then, first thing tomorrow morning I want you to make a stab at getting a pile of my theatre accounts into proper order. My office is on the third floor of the Tiring-House. That is where the important accounting work is done.'

Sally was so overjoyed she ran around the desk and hugged Mr. Burbage, then back again and hugged Toby, then back again to give Mr. Burbage an even bigger hug.

'Thank-you-thank-you, Mr. Burbage, sir,' she repeated. 'You will never know how much this means to me!'

When Inky and Herbert heard the new their gobs were well-and-truly smacked and their flabbers were well-and-truly gasted.

'Imagine!' Herbert said in astonishment. 'You are the first girl ever to work in the Globe, and I do mean *ever!* I-It's unbelievable.'

Back at Puddle Street, Inky's mum, on delivering the promised mutton stew plus a basket of oatcakes *and* a jug of honey, was equally flabbergasted. With a tear in her eye she held Sally firmly by the shoulders.

'In all my born days, my child: I have never known such a thing.' She proudly proclaimed. 'A wee slip of a girl earning money in a man's workplace. I'd take my hat off to you if I had a hat. You will be an inspiration to all girls.' And from that moment on, Sally could do no wrong in the eyes of Mrs. Annie Blyster.

Later on, after his mum's crock of delicious stew and wonderful oatcakes had been entirely devoured, Inky sat up excitedly.

'I've just remembered a fun thing we could do.'

'Yeah, and what's that?' Toby asked.

'Come along and find out. I just need to grab some

plaster-mix first.'

Sally rolled her eyes jokily. 'Can't you just here sit by the fire and continue praising me?'

'We'll get back to that later,' Inky promised. 'This will be good fun.'

Toby and Sally could hardly believe it when Inky led them upstairs and steered them into the little cubbyhole.

'It's an old tradition to write your name inside the roof of a new house,' Inky explained as he smeared wet plaster on a corner wall.

'It's supposed to bring the house good luck.'

As soon as Herbert had scrawled his name on the plaster Toby grabbed the writing stick and very carefully added his name – plus a personal little message to the future.

Herbert Herring
Toby Sprocket (Hi Unc!)
Inky Blyster

Inky scratched his head. *'Hi Unc? What's a Hi Unc?'*

'Ah, it's just an old saying from up north,' Toby explained. 'A sort of greeting, that's all.'

'And what about you, Sally,' Herbert said, wiping mucky plaster from his hands. 'Don't you want to add your name?'

Hunkered down inside that little cubbyhole, a great wave of homesickness washed over Sally's heart. For a few brief seconds her old life felt lovingly close and yet a billion miles away. Smilingly she remembered the first time she saw those names and wondered if maybe, hundreds of years from now, the professor might look at them again and wonder?

'No, no, it's ok. Just stick 1610 on the bottom – and let's get back to that warm fire,' she said quickly, before scurrying out through the little cubbyhole doorway.

An angry wind began whipping the roof, rattling the windows and howling down the chimney. Sally was comforted to be away from all that. Enjoying the company of friends and listening to praise for her exploits was far nicer.

'I was just thinking,' Herbert said eventually. 'Maybe we should warn you about who to keep away from in Southwark.'

'Aye, forewarned is forearmed.' Inky agreed, tapping the side of his nose.

'So listen-up you two,' Herbert continued. 'Right from the giddy-up there is one particular evil blackguard you must avoid like the plague.'

While Herbert and Inky nodded conspiratorially at each other, Toby took their warning far less than seriously.

'Yikes! Is he like, a scary bogeyman?' He said jokingly, wriggling his fingers for comic effect.

The boys were not laughing.

Instead they looked around uneasily as if a pair of ears might suddenly sprout out of the wall. Herbert leaned in close to Toby.

'Toby. Christian Hemlock is no joke. I'm not kidding when I say you must avoid him at all times. He's a whole different kind of evil. Imagine a black-hearted monster who'd cut your head off as quick as spit at you – and you still wouldn't be close to describing him.'

'Avoid....at... all... times,' Inky repeated, jabbing

Toby's chest with each word.

'But why would the Globe employ someone like that?' Sally asked incredulously.

'You've hit the nail right on the head,' said Herbert. 'Hemlock isn't *employed* by anyone. He simply takes what he wants – lock, stock, barrel, and box – usually at the point of a knife or a gun. Right now the Globe is paying him money for its safety.'

'Its safety! Safety from what?'

'From brutes like himself. But of course nobody will ever say that to his face.'

'Which, in a roundabout way, brings us to the question of wages.' Inky said with a sigh. 'Didn't you notice how Burbage neglected to mention pay?'

'To be honest, no,' said Toby. 'I just glad to get a job. But since *you* mention it: why didn't he…?'

'---because Hemlock has been squeezing the Globe for every penny he can get, that's why. As a result our wages are so low we hardly earn enough to live on. Burbage says he can't afford to pay more. And in fairness, we all believe he's telling the truth.'

Like the howling wind outside, the mood inside had become gloomy and ominous. The four friends stared into the fire, and for a while didn't speak

'You know what I think.' Herbert said eventually, grabbing the fireguard and fixing it in front of the fire. 'I think turning-up late on your first day would not be a good plan, especially where old Burbage is concerned. I say we cheer-up, hit the sack, and look forward to tomorrow.'

'And *that's* what I call a plan,' said Sally, jumping to her feet. 'So, good luck, good night, and hope the bed-bugs don't bite.'

*

Later on, stretched out on her mattress, Sally knotted her hands behind her head.

'I can hardly believe what happened to us today, and God *knows* what tomorrow will be like?' she mused, her eyes fixed on the skylight window. 'It's totally bizarre.'

'Bizarre doesn't even come close,' said Toby. 'I mean, finding that notebook was beyond bizarre, more like a miracle. It's going to help us so much. I can feel it.'

'I do hope so, Toby.'

'Sally, getting home is the endgame for us – nothing else matters. And now we can seriously start aiming for that. But first we have this job thing to deal with.'

Sally looked at the Mark 5, and yawned.

'Toby, I know I keep going on about it. But I just cannot get my head around the fact that we are actually going to start working in the Globe theatre.'

For a few tranquil moments they thought about the last twenty-four hours.

'Mutton Stew à la Blyster!' Toby suddenly blurted. And for one joyous minute they quietly laughed themselves silly. Sally laughed so much she fell back and banged her head on the Mark 5, which made them laugh even more.

'One thing's for sure. We'll never go hungry if Inky's mum has anything to do with it.'

'Ok, we had better quieten down,' Toby said, wiping his eyes. 'I have a gut feeling tomorrow will be even bigger than today.'

Sally punched her pillow. 'I don't even want to think about it.'

Toby tucked an arm behind his head. 'Alright then, it's time to make new dreams.'

9. THE GLOBE

Five o'clock Monday morning and an air of feverish excitement buzzed around the Blyster household. Herbert had arrived early to help with breakfast, and it wasn't long until the four pals were gobbling down bowls of steaming hot porridge.

Rushing outside, Sally and Toby had never seen such darkness. In fact they'd never been *awake* at such an ungodly hour. The pitch-black streets were filled with spooky silhouettes that only turned into humans when they passed by. Crossing London Bridge was equally strange. Clunky hob-nail footsteps, chesty coughs and grumpy chatter echoed noisily along the bridge as hundreds of Londoners trundled along in a great hurry to get to their work.

Exiting the bridge the friends turned right and headed east along the quays where boats and ships bobbed on the dark water like giant black slugs.

'Hey you two. We're almost there now,' Inky announced, looking back and pointing ahead.

Minutes later, as sunrise scattered the last remnants of nightfall, a tall building began emerging through the dawn mist. Sally held her breath. With its open thatched roof, shiny black timbers and pristine whitewash, the Globe was everything she dreamed it would be.

'As the old saying goes "Once more unto the breach" dear friends,' Inky said cheerfully, as he pushed through the Globe's big timber entrance doors.

Sally's eyes were busy devouring everything: a crest over the entrance which read "The Whole World is a

Playhouse." Flaming torches that sent shadows bouncing from wall-to-wall, stagehands huffing and puffing as they worked around the apron stage. And last but not least, stretching right around the entire theatre, were those three great audience galleries.

A voice bellowed from a top balcony.

'Hey everyone, look what the cat just dragged in – Blyster and Herring, the laziest dossers in all London.'

It was the voice of Stinky McGinnty, his long pointy face protruding between giant goofy ears. 'And if I'm not too mistaken, they've brought along a nice pair of rookies ready for the plucking.'

A swell of rowdy guffaws rippled through the theatre as men trickled down from galleries and stores to inspect the newcomers. As soon as they set eyes on Sally they were stopped dead in their tracks.

'Blimey, i-it's a girl, in long pants,' declared Mincer Crabtree, a gigantic shaven-headed chap with cross-eyes. It was like he was seeing a female for the first time.

'Bloody hell, Blyster. I know you're getting desperate for a date,' said Stinky McGinnty, scratching one of his giant ears. 'But isn't kidnapping carrying things a bit far, even for you.'

Inky cleared his throat. 'Toby… Sally, in case you're wondering. McGinnty and Crabtree are employed here to frighten away rodents and other associates.'

'Yeah, well. It looks like we failed with you two then.' Mincer said laughingly, poking the side of Inky's head with a stumpy finger.

And even though the men could hardly believe a real live girl would be working alongside them, Toby and Sally were welcomed like long lost cousins. Everyone was exceedingly sociable and friendly, everyone that is, except a creepy galloot who came slithering out from the shadows. In a patched-up overcoat with frayed elbows and missing buttons, and with hair so greasy a gale-force wind wouldn't have shifted it. He looked shifty, squirmy and ridiculous.

'My, my. What have we got here?' he sneered, his mouth slurping as if gnawing on something ungnaw-able. 'Two new chickens for me to keep an eye on, eh.'

'Sid... is that *you?*' Inky gasped, staring with disbelieving eyes at the little thug standing in front of him.

'What's going on, have you gone mad? Is this what Hemlock has you doing now, spying and threatening people?'

Sid Dripping did not appreciate being pulled-up in front of the new arrivals.

'I told you already, Blyster. Nobody makes me do anything. I work for Mr. Hemlock because I like to!'

'Wha... you *like* working for a fiend who would cut your heart out as quick as spit at you. Is that what you're saying?'

'Yeah, that's what I'm saying.'

'Really, you actually *like* that?'

'Are you deaf, I just said I do!'

'There's no hope for you then, is there, Sid?'

'No hope for *you,* you mean!'

'No, for you!'

'No, for YOU....'

Toby had heard enough. 'Hey guys, take it easy,' he smiled. 'And you, Dropping or Drooling or whatever you call yourself. I think you better clear off.'

Toby was so tall, Sid looked a child beside him. But Sid needed to look tough: in fact with the entire Globe workforce watching him, his reputation depended on it.

'How would you like to own a horribly damaged

face?' He growled, his eyes creeping all over Toby.

'Why dude – you selling yours?' Toby said, struggling to stop himself sniggering at this scrawny kid.

The Globe cracked up with laughter. Stinky McGinnty laughed so hard he collapsed. By that stage, Sid, in the face of such embarrassment, and feeling increasingly self-conscious, threw back his bony shoulders and scratched a line on the ground with his foot. '

Step across that and you'll soon find out what I'm selling,' he grinned through yellow teeth. 'Go on, try it. I'll make you bleeeed.'

To back-up the threat, Sid flashed the handle of a huge knife from inside his oversized coat.

'No shit, Sherlock,' Toby replied, chuckling scornfully as he stepped across the line. 'Ok, give it your best shot.'

But before Sid could say or do anything, Sally stepped in.

'Oh for heaven's sake, Toby,' she demanded, angrily pushing Toby away from Sid. 'Can we cut all the macho nonsense. Or do you want to get fired on your first day, because of this… this… grotty little twerp.'

'Oy, mind your lip, girl!' Sid fumed.

'Ignore her, Sid.' Herbert grinned, slapping Sid on the back. 'She's just being accurate.'

Sally was still pushing Toby. 'Enough is enough!'

'Ok Sally, I get it. We're finished now.'

All eyes then turned towards Hemlock's spy.

'Hey you, grotty little twerp guy,' shouted Mincer Crabtree from the back of the theatre. 'Piss off before we let the little girl give you a brand new damaged face.'

A tirade of sniggers, titters and jibes bobbed around the theatre. Poor little Sid. Such a bad-tempered encounter with his old pals left him feeling deeply confused and humiliated. He glanced around apprehensively. Not for the first time did he suspect that working for Hemlock wasn't such a great idea. In desperate need for somewhere to hide, he slithered back into the shadows, and snuck quietly out through a side door of the theatre.

A booming voice made everybody jump. It was Burbage, his roly-poly extravagantly dressed figure toddling out from behind the stage.

'That's exactly what one likes to see. Young people eager to work and make money for the good old GLOBE!' he thundered, laughing heartily at his own joke.

Staring hard at Sally – he puffed out a deep breath. For one horrible moment Sally thought he had forgotten her? She needn't have worried: Burbage raised his big bushy eyebrows and smiled sweetly.

'Good morning, Miss Dunn.'

Sally swallowed. 'Eh, its Bunn actually, sir.' She said nervously.

'Bunn. Exactly.' Burbage sniffed. 'As I informed you yesterday: although you demonstrated excellent abilities for mathematics. You still need to prove you're smart enough to look after some real accounting concerns. Run along now to my office, and we shall soon find out how you operate in the real world.'

'And as for you, Master Sprocket. We shall also find out if hard work is to your taste.'

Toby summoned-up a nuclear-powered smile of confidence.

'Hard work is always to my taste, Mr. Burbage,' he said.

'Excellent. I shall leave you in the capable hands of

our foreman here, Mr. Mullion. Pay attention to what he has to say and you will have no difficulties.'

Growler Mullion, a muscular pointy-headed man, six foot-something at least, with eyes like brown marbles and a face that would frighten a wolf, stepped out from behind Burbage.

Toby scanned the great stack of muscle and sinew standing in front of him. 'Now that is one scary looking dude...' he thought to himself, smiling apprehensively.

Inky, Herbert, Stinky and Mincer, were avidly watching events unfold.

'And what do you four bampots want?' Burbage snapped. '....early retirement perhaps?'

Inky cleared his throat. 'N-No sir---'

'.... well then shoo, shoo, get back to your work before I take a stick to the lot of you.'

'Excuse me, Mr. Burbage, sir.' Growler Mullion said, his toothless mouth struggling to get the words out. I have a question afore you go?'

'Something wrong, Mullion?'

'Aye sir, there is. It's this 'ere wages situation with the workers. They asked me say that feelings are running high, and---'

'...Mister Mullion. As I've said to you many times before. I dearly wish I could help, I really do. But we simply do not have the money. Matters might improve after our new production, but until then there is not much else I can say on the matter. I am truly sorry.'

'We understand your position, sir. But---'

'The answer still has to be no, Mr. Mullion. As I have said, maybe after our new production.' Whereupon Burbage turned and speedily headed off towards his own workrooms.

With a face like a bag of spanners, Growler Mullion

turned his attention to a scared looking Toby.

'There is only one rule here you need to learn: never ask stupid questions and always do what I tell you!'

'...but...that's...two rules.'

Growler Mullion glared at Toby like an upset demon. '...and the *second* rule is, never be a know-it-all. Got that?'

'Got that, sir!'

'Good,' the foreman barked. 'Now, go fetch me a left-handed screwdriver.'

'A-A left-handed screwdriver, you say...' Toby stuttered, looking around confusedly.

'And while you're at it, I'll also be needing a glass hammer. One with a pink handle should do the trick.'

'Okay... a glass hammer with a pink handle, and a left-handed screwdriver?' Toby muttered, his eyes darting about in a rising panic.

It was when hoots of laughter poured down from every corner of the theatre that Toby suspected he might be the butt of a joke.

'Okay, I get it,' he laughed. 'Glass hammers, left-handed screw drivers, hardy-har-har.'

'You'll do all right, lad,' Growler Mullion declared with a smile. 'Come along, follow me.'

Leading Toby out through the main doors, the foreman nodded towards a cart full of logs and planks.

'Unload – one hour – no stopping,' he growled.

'That's fine, no problem, don't worry about it,' Toby was casually insisting. 'But eh... I was wondering if I might take a short teabreak? Like I'm *sooo* not used to getting up before dawn, I really could do with a breather.'

Mullion stared at Toby as if he'd just sprouted an extra head. Frowning, he cupped his hands around his mouth, and at the top of his voice shouted into Toby's face.

'UNload...ONE hour...NO STOPPING.'

'Yes sir, no stopping sir, one hour!' Toby quickly replied, stepping away with a hand raised in surrender.

Up to that point in his life Toby had successfully avoided all forms of physical labour. For that reason it didn't take long for his body to ache all over and be drenched in sticky sweat. Annoyingly, about an hour into this agonising assignment, he could feel someone's eyes boring into him. Quickly cheesed-off by this intrusion he was about to give the nosey parker a piece of his mind, when a friendly voice broke the silence.

'Excuse me, young sir?' the voice said.

Flinging a bunch of timbers to the ground, Toby wiped his sweaty face with his sleeve, and glared at the meddlesome stranger.

'What's up, doc?' he grumbled.

'Ehh... nothing is up, as far as I know,' the stranger answered blankly. 'I merely wish to ask you a question.'

'Sure, what the hell... fire away.'

'Perhaps I should introduce myself first. My name is Shakespeare, William Shakespeare.'

10. MR. S

Leaning his head to one side, Toby rubbed his chin as if figuring something out.

'William Shakespeare? Like... William Shakespeare, the guy who wrote all those plays and stuff?'

Mr. Shakespeare arched an eyebrow. 'Yes, I have written plays... and stuff!'

'Cool, it's really good to meet you,' Toby smiled, wiping grime from his hand on a trouser leg and then holding it out. 'My name is Toby Sprocket.'

Removing a leather glove, Shakespeare took Toby's hand.

'How do you do, Master Sprocket.'

'All things considered, I'm doing ok. And eh... sorry for being grumpy just now,' Toby apologised. 'But you would not *believe* the last couple of days I've had. Completely knackered hardly comes close.'

Shakespeare pressed a finger to his chin. 'Knackered? That is a word I have not heard before. What is its meaning?'

'It's like... feeling wasted.' Toby explained, shaking his head and looking thoughtful. 'Or exhausted maybe?'

'I take my hat off to you, Master Sprocket. I know you less than a minute and already I have learned something.'

Before Toby could even begin to appreciate the fact that he had just taught William Shakespeare a new word – he took notice of his dashing attire. There was a navy-blue cloak draped over his left shoulder, a snazzy pair of leather boots rising right up to his knees, and a neatly trimmed hipster beard on a face accustomed to lots of smiling. A gold earring in his right ear completed the fancy get-up.

'I am looking for a strong dependable lad to stick posters up around town...' Mr. Shakespeare continued – his eyes, bright sharp and blue. 'It's a brainchild of Mr. Burbage: he believes it might help to generate extra interest in our upcoming new play *The Winter's Tale*.'

At which point he plonked a bucket of paste and a big hairy brush in front of Toby.

'I should say that at first some of his schemes sound a bit odd: like using flags to advertise particular plays – they do usually work out in the end. So there you have it, Master Sprocket. Might you be interested? I have cleared it already with Burbage.'

'Are you kidding?' Toby said, his face lighting up. 'Of course I'm interested.'

'Excellent. I shall go through the procedures with you. Do you have any questions before we start?'

'Just the one,' Toby ventured, as his belly made a loud churgling-gurgling noise. 'What happens if I die from hunger?'

Worried he may have overstepped the mark, Toby inwardly flinched. His new boss exhaled a quick chuckle and shook his head.

'I take it you are perhaps, a little peckish?'

'More than just a little!' said Toby. 'I'd eat the hind leg off an angry bull if I could catch one.'

Laughing louder this time, Toby's new boss slapped him on the back. 'Let us go catch a bull then.'

'Un-friggin-real' Toby thought, when five minutes later he was tucking into a mammoth-sized cheese sandwich with Mr. S (Toby's nickname for Shakespeare) in a tavern. And before their impromptu snack was

finished they were chit-chatting like they'd known each other for years.

'I just thought of something,' Shakespeare announced between mouthfuls. 'Burbage informs me that you and your cousin are from up north. I was wondering, where exactly? Perhaps we may know some people. I have many acquaintances and relatives in both Manchester and Leeds.'

Toby gulped. This was the one subject he wanted to stay as far away from as possible.

'Eh, well, the thing is, you see, Sally and I are not actually from Manchester or Leeds.'

'That is a pity. And where do you hail from?'

'Em, do you know anyone from say... York?' Toby asked meekly.

Shakespeare thought for a moment. 'Hmm, no. Not that I can recall.'

'Phew! I mean, tut-tut... that *is* a pity: because that's where we're from. York, I mean. Lovely town is York. Lovely jubbly.'

'Well, Master Sprocket from lovely-jubbly-York. Time waits for no man. So I trust, now that you have eaten, I can leave you to your own devices. you will work hard for the rest of the day. Perhaps tomorrow we might check if the posters are still up?'

'No probs,' said Toby. 'I'll be looking forward to that as well.'

'Good,' said Shakespeare, pulling on his cape. 'Let us get you started.'

It was no easy job lugging around a big bucket of paste and slapping up posters in cold weather. Still, regardless of the hard work, it was fantastic for Toby to experience the sights, the sounds and the reality of old London, knowing he had somewhere safe to sleep. The sun shone brighter, dead leaves skittling along the ground sounded less lonely, and the sheer terror of being stuck in the past was forgotten.

By the time Toby got back to the Globe, gossip was flying about how the new kid nabbed the most coveted of jobs.

'You lucky swine,' Inky declared, chasing Toby down. 'I've been sucking-up to old Shaky for months. And you saunter along and nab it in one day. How? I mean *how?'*

'Well – at first I thought it might have been my mesmerizing charm and good looks.' Toby explained. 'But as it turns out… it *was* my mesmerizing charm and good looks!'

'Yeah, or maybe you're just a good brown-noser.'

'You might be right, Inky.' Toby laughed. 'Seriously though. Having a job and paying my way is all that matters.'

'You're certainly doing that, my northern friend. But it's nothing compared to what Sally has done!'

'What's she done – is everything ok?'

'Ok! Try *perfectly* ok! She was amazing. Wait till you hear what happened…'

11. SALLY'S BIG DAY

Sally stared goggle-eyed at the higgledy-piggledy stacks of files piled high in the room Mr. Burbage called his 'office'. Hardly big enough for two people to stand in, it was so small and stuffy, specks of dust swirled through the air like little grey atoms.

'The pile on the left is for payments coming in,' Mr. Burbage explained. 'And the bigger pile on the right mostly concern payments going out. I'm hoping against hope you can arrange them into some kind of...of...'

'---systematic order?' Sally suggested.

Burbage nodded approvingly.

'Yes. Yes. Systematic order. I *do* like the sound of that.'

'I'll begin straightaway then, shall I?' Sally offered, fixing her eyes on the paper piles.

'I was thinking (cough) that perhaps you might prefer to be left to your own devices?' Burbage suggested. 'With me out of the way.... perhaps?'

'Actually, Mr. Burbage. That would be a help.'

'Say no more, my child. I shall return in the afternoon,' he said, much relieved. 'Let the trial begin.'

As soon as Mr. Burbage had bolted out the door, Sally dived into her work like a conscientious robot. Dusting, tidying, arranging and cleaning, she didn't stop until everything was ship-shape and spick-and-span. Her next job was actually less complicated since it involved straightforward bookkeeping – which, thanks to her dad's excellent tutoring, she could tackle with ease.

Later on, when examining a specific bunch of papers,

Sally sat back with a confused look on her face.

'Now that is odd?' she said quietly, her eyes widening. 'Odd in the extreme.'

It was late afternoon before Mr. Burbage returned.

'My word!' he gasped with delight. 'What has happened here? It looks absolutely amazing: like a new room.'

Sally's mouth opened as if to answer, but turning red-faced and bashful, she snapped it shut again.

'Seriously, my dear. This is most impressive. Why, you have even sharpened my quills!' he exclaimed, holding a bundle of goose feathers up to the light. 'Very impressive indeed. And no doubt you have arranged the accounts in a 'systematic order' as well?'

'Well yes, Mr. Burbage. The books have been arranged as we discussed. But I do have a couple of questions regarding certain accounts.

'Fire away, my girl, fire away,' Burbage repeated, holding his hands behind his back while bobbing up-and-down on the spot.

Sally flicked through a bunch of papers. 'Ah yes, here we are,' she continued, locating a file. 'Who are Sedgely Brothers, Silas Harvey, and Messer's Fling & Hopplecoat?'

'Hmm, let me think now?' said Burbage, tapping a finger on his lips.

'Oh yes, I remember. Mr. Harvey's company re-thatched the roof following a little fire about three years ago. Fling & Hopplecoat are the painters we used at that time – and the Sedgely Brothers made those wonderful new front doors last year. Why do you ask?'

'Because according to these accounts you've been continuously paying them every week since then.'

Burbage's face went snow white. 'No, no, no, that

can't be right!' he spluttered, grabbing the papers from Sally. 'I mean, we *couldn't*, could we?'

'Don't worry, Mr. Burbage.' Sally said reassuringly. 'You haven't... not really. You simply forgot to take their names off your weekly payment records. In fact, according to my research, the Globe is approximately £283 better off.'

'I don't quite follow?'

'Well, in plain English, there is approximately £283 slushing about in your accounts that you didn't know about.'

In shock, Burbage slouched down onto a chair. 'Are you certain about this, I mean absolutely certain? £283 is a small fortune. Have you checked with Goldsmiths – our banking people?'

'Oh yes,' Sally said confidently. 'I have double-checked with everything. I may be a couple of pounds out either way, but there is no doubting what has happened *and* that the money is still 'safe' within the company funds.'

'Astonishing! Amazing! Astounding!' Burbage jumped to his feet, flipping through the papers and grinning from ear-to-ear. 'Sally, do you have any idea what this means?'

'Not really,' Sally replied calmly. 'But I'm sure it's mostly good news.'

Burbage laughed. 'Mostly good news, she says! It changes everything around here. Come along now, child. We need to announce these good tidings.'

Hugely excited, Burbage grabbed Sally by the hand and charged out from the office. Moments later they were standing at the centre of the Globe stage.

'Attention everybody please! Could you all gather round. Come along now, quickly!' Burbage shouted. 'I have important news for you all. Come along now and pay attention.'

The banging and the hammering and the pulling and lifting gradually came to a halt as worried-looking workers dragged themselves towards the stage.

'Oh-oh,' Inky whispered to Herbert. 'Do you think Sally has done something terribly wrong? Is she going to get the sack?'

'Don't think so. I mean, have you ever seen old Burbage smiling so much.'

'I shall come straight to the point.' Burbage resumed at the top of his voice. 'The Globe Theatre Company is happy to announce that from this week onwards every one of you shall have a three penny rise in your wages. Not a fortune, I know. But in appreciation for all your hard work and your patience through this difficult period, you shall also have a special day off tomorrow. And if you are wondering, which I'm sure you are, how this miracle has come about – look no further than this young lady, Miss Sally Bunn.'

Burbage stood aside to reveal a blushing Sally.

'With her wondrous work on the ledgers and account books,' Burbage went on. 'She alone made this possible. We owe her our thanks and our gratitude.'

For a long moment stunned silence reigned as twenty-nine working men stared dumbfoundedly at their unlikely financial saviour. Inky and Herbert broke the silence by bursting into a rousing cheer. Everybody wholeheartedly joined in.

'Please,' Sally mumbled, her face now full-on crimson. 'I-I was only doing my job.'

At that point the cheering and applause became even louder.

This was the final straw for a mortified Sally. 'Oh

dear,' she mumbled, before she ran back to the safety of the office.

With the hum of joyful conversation rolling around the theatre, Burbage shouted again.

'Right men, come along, back to work. Your day off is *tomorrow* not today.'

Hurrying back after Sally, Burbage gave her the news she desperately wanted to hear.

'Sally my dear, you have passed with flying colours. You are now officially Head Clerk of Ledgers and Accounts for the Globe Theatre. And for a special bonus you can take the rest of the day off as *well* as tomorrow.'

Minutes later, as Sally discreetly left the theatre, she was confronted by a reverential parade of co-workers who bowed and nodded and praised as she passed by.

'Good day to you, Miss Sally'... 'Look after yourself, now'... 'See you on Wednesday, Miss Sally'... 'Mind how you go, Miss Sally...'

Last in line was a smiling Inky and Herbert, doffing imaginary caps and performing an especially intricate curtsy.

'Will her ladyship be sampling the royal stew at her Puddle Street residence this evening?' Inky snootily inquired.

'Thank you, guys,' she whispered, wrapping Inky and Herbert in a hug. 'This could not have happened without your help. I mean it. So thank you – thank you – thank you, for everything!'

Later that evening it was celebration time in Puddle Street.

'Here's the feast we promised earlier, Sally.' Herbert announced, while carefully placing a steaming pot of Mrs. Blyster's mega-stew on the dining table.

'Cheers to the hero of the moment,' said Toby, raising

a mug of cold milk to Sally. 'And let's hope our day off will be filled with even more fun and surprises. Cheers!'

'And to think we tried to put you off applying for the job!' said Herbert, raising his mug.

Bowls were filled and spoons were readied, and before long the sound slurping, glugging, and scoffing filled the room. Soon after, with bellies filled and darkness painting the windows, it was time for a jolly chin-wag. Jokes were laughed at, tall-tales were blabbed and the crazy goings-on at the Globe were marvelled over.

'And what about that ridiculous looking Sid guy,' Toby hooted. 'Talk about goofy!'

Inky and Herbert exchanged a look.

'Hey, I'm sorry, guys? Toby said in mock surprise. 'Have I said something wrong?'

'Ach, it's not your fault, Toby. It's just painful for us to see what's happened to Sid.' Inky sadly explained.

Herbert nodded in agreement. 'And I know we should see Sid as he is today and not as he was in the past. But it's very hard, Toby. He was once a great friend, our honorary brother – and a close one at that.'

In the doleful silence that followed, Sally backpedalled through her thoughts and feelings.

'There is something you might not have noticed, guys: and I'm not just saying it to make you feel better. But I got the distinct impression that Sid's heart wasn't really in it. All that hard-man stuff. It felt like an act. And a bad one at that.'

'Sally is on to something there.' Toby said. 'It felt like he didn't know how to be a tough-guy. Maybe he's regretting things and missing his real friends. Honestly, I don't think you've heard the last of him yet.'

Herbert stood up to leave. 'That's very nice of you to

say, Toby. And while none of us know what the future may hold, we don't really have much hope for Sid.'

'Well best not dwell on it, then.' said Sally. 'If we want to fully enjoy our day off tomorrow, I think we all need a good night's rest.'

'I'll second that!' Herbert cheered, shucking-on his coat and waving goodnight.

'And I'll third it!' laughed Inky, slapping his friend on the back.

*

Later that night, when Inky's snores trumbled round the house, a muffled activity had started-up in the attic. With Professor Sprockett's notebook in hand and a candle flickering atop the Mark 5, Toby pulled open the engine cover and shoved his head into the belly of the machine. Very carefully he began disconnecting components and parts, and after he and Sally had checked, cleaned, and polished each piece, he just as carefully reconnected them.

'Toby, I don't want to be a downer but what if the problem is not with the engine – what if it's something else?'

'Well then, you'll have to come-up with another Sally Bunn miracle.'

'I'm being serious, Toby.'

'So am I. I mean, wasn't it *you* who kick-started our escape from Dungworth. And wasn't it *you* who found Unc's notebook: which is absolutely priceless. And also, wasn't it *you* who conjured-up a pay rise *and* got us a day off tomorrow. None of that was accidental.'

'I already told you. None of it was planned either. It just happened.'

'Unc always says nothing just happens. It is paying proper attention to what's going on around you that makes the difference. And paying attention is what you do fantastically well.'

Sally shrugged. 'Yes.... Well... since you put it that way. I suppose I am brilliant at most things.'

'Not...so...sure that's what I said, little Miss Bighead?'

'Well, it's what I heard. And now I don't want to talk about it anymore.'

An hour later Sally was working so hard her head slouched down until her chin was almost touching the engine parts. Toby watched with concern as she carried on without complaint.

'You ok to keep going?' he asked.

'Absolutely. And you were right about this cleaning, some of the parts are quite dirty.'

As the flickering candle cast shadows around the attic, another hour passed in silence. Eventually Sally, tired-out, sat back against the wall.

'Can I ask you something, Toby?'

'Sure you can'

'Well, I was just thinking... when you step outside that little attic door, does it feel like you become a completely different person?'

Toby thought for a moment. 'Yeah kinda, I suppose. But it's more like I borrow someone else's mindset for a while. And when I get back here, I become myself again. It's how my brain deals with what's happening to us, I guess.'

'That's exactly how I feel.' Sally nodded slowly. 'It's like we transform ourselves on a daily basis just to stay sane.'

'Exactly.'

'So, you *do* then!'

'I do what then?'

'Become a completely different person… beyond the attic door?'

'Nah. That's just crazy girl talk.'

Sally whacked him with her cleaning cloth. 'I do mean what I'm saying, you great twit!'

'I know you do, Sal. It's just good to hear you laugh.'

As a lash of rain peppered the tiny window again and a swirling wind whistled across the roof, Toby leaned on the machine.

'You know what I really think, Sally?'

'No, what?'

'I think we've become like, fighters. Creators of our own destiny.'

'You know, Toby. Even though that sounds really cool and inspirational. I'm fast becoming a very tired little creator of destiny. I'm seeing double I'm so bushed.'

'Me too.' Toby yawned. 'But I am so glad we finally got to make a start on the machine. It feels like we're really fighting back – doing something constructive.'

Sally blew out the candle. And when the wind and the rain began to loosen their grip. Everything started to feel ok. They lay there peacefully for a while, until bit-by-bit they felt their eyes closing. One minute later they were sound asleep.

12. DARK DOINGS

Mr. Shakespeare never liked being outdoors on cold winter evenings. And on that particularly cold winter evening, as frost coated the city like dusty white sugar, he disliked it even more. Most of all he disliked the creature sitting behind a small desk in front of him. Christian Hemlock, his face all flushed and blotchy, looked more monstrous than usual. His one good eye, the right one, was icy-grey and all-seeing, while the left one, the one made from the blackest crystal, conveyed a look of pure evil. In the flickering candle-light it changed colour – darkest purple to hellish greens and browns, and then back to purest black.

Ignoring that demonic eye as best as he could, Shakespeare grappled to find a pocket inside layers of capes and coats. In due course he hauled out a small cotton bag that contained thirty silver coins. It jingled when he chucked it on an old mahogany desk.

'I'm not sure we can afford this amount every week,' Shakespeare began earnestly, giving his tormentor a placatory look. 'Perhaps it is time to discuss new terms?'

Fixing his attention momentarily on the money-bag, Hemlock drummed his long fingernails on the desk.

'My dear man,' he began in a scornful voice, looking above and beyond Shakespeare as if he were a pesky nuisance. 'If I had a penny for every time I heard that, I'd be as rich as a king.'

Shakespeare hesitated. 'Be that as it may, sir. I assure you these payments cannot be sustained.'

Hemlock yawned as if Shakespeare was the most

boring man in the world. Slouching back he coldly observed the distress on his victim's face.

'Please – take a seat,' he said smilingly, his oddly pointed teeth glinting in the candlelight.

Taking a flagon of whiskey from a drawer he filled two small tumblers. He pushed one towards Shakespeare.

'To the future,' he said, raising his tumbler and gulping his drink down in one swig.

Revulsion rippled through Shakespeare. Faking a sip he pushed the tumbler aside.

'I am being quite sincere, Mr. Hemlock---'

'...sincere, you say!' Hemlock laughed, cutting across Shakespeare. 'Well then, allow me to be just as sincere.'

Hemlock leaned in closer and launched into a blustering anger-filled rant, banging the desk and jabbing a finger like an outraged bully.

'Do you have any idea how expensive it is to protect the business interests of Southwark? Well! Do you? No. You don't, is the answer.' He waved his hand dismissively.

'Furthermore, not for one second do I believe things are as bad as you claim. People are still flocking to the Globe and paying good money for the privilege!

Feigning nonchalance, Shakespeare calmly stated:

'Mr. Hemlock. We don't have a play on every day. Yet we still must pay our people, regardless. There simply isn't enough money to run the theatre and therefore we cannot afford to pay you any more protection money than we already do.'

'Pahh! I also must pay my people. Take my operatives for instance. Before this week is out, one of them will be on guard within the very environs of your theatre just to keep a helpful eye on things. If scallywags or troublemakers were to suddenly threaten the Globe or any of your employees, he would rush to inform me. And that is when you would get your moneys-worth, believe you me. I deal very harshly with troublemakers and scallywags and it's foolhardy in the extreme for you to have any second thoughts about our arrangements. Of course, you are free to change your mind. Though I shudder to think of the consequences.'

And there it was again.

Always the same.

That unspoken threat of deadly violence.

While Hemlock unleashed yet another abusive tirade, Shakespeare studied the pair of hoodlums skulking behind their master. The larger of the two was a knobbly headed individual with a snub nose and a protruding chin. He was more like a sorrowful ape than any human. The other much smaller chap he recognized: it was Sid Dripping, a former employee at the Globe. Shakespeare gazed at Sid's gloomy face and emaciated body. He looked like a badly dressed goblin. Feeling Shakespeare's burning gaze, Sid's head tilted forward, his eyes fixing on the rubbish-strewn floor.

Hemlock concluded his rant, pushed his chair back from the desk, rested his hand on the dagger he always bore on his waist, and snorted like a pig.

'You are a clever man, Mr. Hemlock,' Shakespeare stated dejectedly. 'So you must know that just because something shines, does not make it gold.'

'Aye, Shakespeare. I am a clever man, and people would do well to remember that. I also decide for myself if something is gold or just shiny. I'm quite good at that.'

With lips pulled tight and eyebrows pinched, Hemlock stared intensely at Shakespeare.

'Of course, there is always that other option to consider. You know, the option where you freely invite me to handle day-to-day matters at the Globe, thus allowing you and Mr. Burbage get on with what you do best: writing and acting and being all artistic. Never again would you have to worry about troublemakers or exorbitant wage demands. And, of course, I would continue to pay everyone a fair wage. How seriously have you thought about those advantages?'

Shakespeare was aghast at Hemlock's never-ending desire to either rule or destroy everything he doesn't already own.

'As I have told you many times, Mr. Hemlock. Handing over control of the Globe is a request we simply cannot agree to. The answer is still no.'

Hemlock, flushed with anger, scratched his stubbly chin – it sounded like sandpaper.

'This meeting is concluded. You should go.' Hemlock barked, while pouring himself another drink. 'We will talk again about my offer. Although, by that stage, I might not be so compassionate.'

Standing to take his leave, Shakespeare looked at Sid Dripping who in turn began fidgeting and pulling at his threadbare shirt collar.

'I suppose the Globe should be grateful for having a sentinel like Master Dripping watching over us,' Shakespeare remarked while buttoning-up his cape.

Hemlock looked askance at the fidgeting Sid. He tried not to laugh. 'A sentinel…yes.' He smirked. 'That's one way to describe him.'

'Which reminds me. Perhaps it might be better if our young sentinel here, brought the payments directly to me in future. It would save time for everyone, don't you think?'

Shakespeare tensed with suppressed anger. Here was this evil monster, doling out his so-called advice as easily as he doled out death and terror. Hemlock was truly merciless when it came to getting what he wanted. For him slaughter and murder was part of his everyday routine.

Shakespeare sighed and nodded his head. 'Yes, I can see how that might save time for everyone,'

Realising he had just been dismissed, a forlorn Shakespeare departed that dreadful place. In near complete darkness he walked along the grassy banks of the Thames where reeds grew thickly on the sloping verges. Depressing thoughts filled his mind as he pondered Hemlock's words. How had he, like so many others, fallen so easily into that viper's nest? How was it possible that he and Burbage, after all their years of hard work, were now so close to losing it all?

Something else deeply worried him. London, unbelievably, was fast losing her power to excite him. This great city, this place that he loved so dearly was starting to feel ever-so-lonely and overflowing with danger. And finally, on top of everything else, the safety of the people working at the Globe was becoming a serious concern. It was time to discuss new tactics with Burbage: it was time to make painful decisions.

13. A GOOD MORNING

'*Mrs. Blys*ter!' Sally beamed as she kafumbled her way into the kitchen and saw what can only be described as a breakfast-y feast: eggs, bacon, fried mushrooms, pancakes, toast, blackberry jam, the whole shebang and loads of it.

'My Oh My, this looks amazing---' Sally started in excitement.

But before she could finish, Annie Blyster was rushing over to smother her with big motherly hugs.

'I heard all about your latest exploits,' she began, tears of pride welling in her eyes. 'In fact every woman I know has heard about what happened yesterday. First you get a real job, then you get everyone a raise, and to top it all, you get everyone a day off. People can hardly believe it! Actually, until I assure them otherwise, they hardly believe you exist at all.'

'I forgot to warn you,' explained Inky. 'Mum heard all about what you did, Sally, and decided to cook you a special celebratory breakfast.'

'What!' Toby jokingly exclaimed as he arrived into the kitchen behind Sally. '*Sally* gets a special celebratory breakfast? I did stuff too, you know.'

'Of course you did. And aren't you a fine big hero for doing it,' said Mrs. Blyster, carefully piling scrambled eggs, sausages and crispy bacon onto Sally's buttered toast as she took her place at the table. 'But it's this wee girl here who deserves a medal.

'That is so sweet of you, Mrs. Blyster,' Sally chuckled. 'And I don't know how you do it, but your food just gets better and better.'

'Why thank you, my dear. And I don't know how *you* do it? You're a role model for all us women and the whole country will know about you before too long.'

'Oh, it was nothing…'

'---*and* never-ever belittle what you've achieved, my girl. There will be plenty of begrudgers out there who will gladly do that for you. You've done brilliantly, and don't you forget it! Now, with all that said, the day is not getting any shorter and I have work to do. So tuck in and enjoy.'

While still chatting and giggling, Mrs. Blyster noisily loaded-up her cooking utensils and headed for the front door.

'Mum, you're a saint. And thanks for the great brekki,' Inky cheerfully yelled. 'Thank you again, Mrs. Blyster. And goodbye!' Sally called after her.

'And goodbye to you, my dear. *And* no doubt you'll have another great day today,' Annie Blyster answered, just before she closed the door behind her with a thud.

Quickly finishing-off her fantastically delicious breakfast, Sally brushed breadcrumbs from her clothes.

'This whole Globe thing is getting embarrassing and stupid,' she said, slightly red-faced.'

'And what did you expect,' Herbert said. 'Everyone at the Globe is convinced your next trick is to sprout angel wings and fly out the roof.'

'Pfft!' Sally said dismissively, pushing her empty plate away. 'I want to stop talking about all that now, because I have something far more interesting to say *and* I want you both to pay attention.'

With barely contained excitement, she asked a question. 'Guess who'll be calling to my office next week?'

Toby hardly raised an eyebrow and Inky continued devouring his brekki.

'Come on guys, play along… guess who's calling to my office next week?'

'Sally, we've just been through the toughest few days of our lives,' Toby moaned. 'Can't you just tell us?'

'Oh alright, spoilsport. It's William Shakespeare!' she blurted, her fingers spiking out with excitement. 'Like, can you believe that? I mean, can you just *believe* that?'

'Yeah, cool, I suppose,' said Toby, scraping the last of the scrambled egg from his plate.

'Cool…? You suppose?' Sally gasped in disbelief. 'Don't you morons know who I'm talking about?'

'Course we know who you're talking about,' Inky huffed. 'We had a drink with Mr. S only yesterday. Isn't that right, Toby?'

'That we did,' Toby agreed sighing. 'And I have to say, working with Mr. S is far more interesting than I imagined it would be: considering how much I disliked reading his stuff in school.'

'Yeah, much more interesting,' aped Inky, who was such a devotee of Toby by then, he agreed with virtually everything Toby said.

Sally was so dumbstruck it took a few seconds to respond.

'Hold it right there!' she demanded, pointing a finger at Toby's face. 'Mr. S! … Mr. S!… Are you actually telling me that this *Mr. S* person, the one you've been jabbering on about all week, is actually William Shakespeare. Is *that* what you're telling me?

'Uh-huh, sure,' Toby nodded. 'But like, what's the big deal? I thought you'd see him every day up in your fancy-schmancy office.'

'Well obviously not, since I'm only seeing him sometime soon.'

'Ok then, sorry,' said Toby, contritely. 'Tell you what, though. Maybe I could introduce you.'

'Are you deaf? Did I not just tell you I'm meeting him myself?'

'Oh yeah, that's right. Sorry again,' Toby said coyly. 'I wasn't really paying attention.'

Sally's eyes bulged. 'Maybe this will help you concentrate!' she said, grabbing Toby by the ear and pinching it with all her might.

'Ooooouch! Oooooouch! Ooooouch!' Toby squealed like a bag of cats. 'I'm really sorry, Sal – please let go.'

'Toby Sprocket. If this story of yours about meeting *Mr. S* is one of your stupid jokes, I swear you'll be missing an ear.'

'…and I swear it's not a joke.' Toby vowed, gingerly rubbing his throbbing earlobe. 'I met Mr. S that first day, just before lunch. I did tell you about it… remember?'

'But you never said he was William Shakespeare, you blockhead. I mean to say, you are personally acquainted with the greatest playwright in the history of the entire world, and you never thought to tell me?'

'Humph…what all the fuss is about,' Inky piped-up. 'Sure he writes nice words and all, but 'tis the actors who do the real hard work.'

Sally's eyes were just starting to burn into Inky's head when Herbert, his nose blue with the cold, made a noisy entrance.

'Brrrr… now that's what I call hunching-up weather,' he said shiveringly, shucking off his jacket and rubbing his hands in front of the fire. 'And by the way, if you lot are up for it, there's something interesting you might want to see today.'

'Go on then, tell us,' Sally said. 'Anything is better than listening to these two idiots.'

'Tyburn Hill,' Herbert said brightly, rotating his backside towards the fire. 'One of Hemlock's gang is for the chopping block. I thought we might want to go and see the action?'

Sally looked at him in disbelief. 'Do you mean an actual beheading?'

'Yes, of course I mean an actual beheading. You can hardly have a 'pretend' beheading.'

Sally laughed forcefully. 'Herbert, what in heavens name made you think I would ever want to see some poor wretch getting his head chopped off?'

'No-no-no… sorry, let me to explain,' Herbert chortled. 'Hemlock has let it be known, far and wide, that he intends to get the condemned man released scot-free in front of everybody. It's his way of demonstrating just how powerful he has become.'

'So let's get this straight,' Sally said, still dubious. 'There will be no chopping heads off.'

'Not if Hemlock has anything to do with it. And since he has personally put the word out, he's obliged to back it up. Looking stupid is not something he's known for.'

Sally looked questioningly at Toby.

'Could be an interesting experience,' Toby shrugged. 'And since nobody is going to get hurt, maybe we should go for it?'

Sally had become so good at acting like a tough 17th century teenager, she sometimes forgot where she really came from. Her true character was never far from the surface and, no matter what Herbert or Toby said, she could hardly bring herself to get excited about Tyburn. But rather than disappoint everybody she decided to play along.

'Ok then,' she sighed, 'let's grab our coats.'

14. TYBURN

The minute she reached the hallway Sally had begun to regret agreeing to the ugly excursion.

'What is it with the male species?' she asked, seriously. 'Why do you always find horrible situations so very interesting.'

'What are you talking about?' said Toby. 'What horrible situations?'

'Tyburn! Executions! Death!'

'Sal, you don't have to go if you don't want to. It's not mandatory. And remember: no one is actually going to lose their head.'

Sally hesitated.

'Yeah, I do know that. It's just... I had a really bad dream last night, full of hatchets and knives and chopping. So I'm feeling a bit creeped out already and not in the humour for real-life nasty stuff.'

'Well, according to Herbert, there won't be anything nasty. So try not to worry.'

Herbert called from the open front door. 'I always said you can't beat London when it comes to fun!' he declared enthusiastically. 'Come along you two. You won't believe the crowds already going there. And I forgot to tell you there's a funfair as well.'

Diving straight into the flow of people, the four friends were soon on their merry way towards Tyburn. Half an hour later the happy-clappy multitudes were converging across a great open hill. It was so jam-packed the very air tasted of mud and sweat and fried food. Tents and marquees of every size and colour were already there

– circling the hill like a huge canvas horseshoe.

'Awesome or what!' said Toby gawking at troupes of acrobats, minstrels, and food sellers. 'All that's missing is a bouncy castle!'

'It is pretty cool!' Sally nodded approvingly.

'Quick!' said Inky. 'That's a nice little grassy area just over there.'

As soon as they commandeered the grassy knoll, the fun suddenly stopped for Toby and Sally. Way down at the front of the crowded hill they saw the execution scaffold, grotesquely adorned with strings of black ribbon and painted bright red and blue. It looked like a cross between a pantomime stage and a helicopter landing pad.

'Now that is creepy,' Sally said in a low voice.

'And I bet that chopping block doesn't get many laughs either,' Toby said, nodding towards a chunk of wood in the middle of the scaffold floor.

On cue ponderous drumbeats began to approach the field. As the drumbeats got nearer, the mood of the crowd changed from good-humoured to grumpy-hostile. For a minute it reminded Toby of a riotous Chelsea home game just before kick-off.

'What's happening, guys, what's with the drums?' Sally shouted, standing on her tippy-toes for a better view.

'It's the prisoner on a horse and cart.' Herbert yelled, pointing over the heads of the noisy crowd. 'Look, he's at the scaffold now.'

Between militiamen and a hunchback official dressed in shabby robes, stood a man, shouting and roaring, his arms tied firmly behind his back. An ugly scar ran from his left ear to his top lip, locking his mouth in a permanent sneer.

'Agggggh… a pox on the lot of you!' he howled. 'Rot in hell I say!'

Like a swarm of vultures a great press of spectators pushed forward yelling and waving their fists. Sally, who never liked crowds regardless of the occasion, squeezed her eyes shut and pressed her head into Toby's arms.

'Please can we leave now,' she pleaded in a choking voice. 'I really don't want to be here anymore.'

'Sorry, Sal. We can't leave now. It's too packed. Don't worry though, we don't have to watch.'

A frenzy of hissing and booing assailed the prisoner as he was dragged kicking and screaming from the cart. The more he bawled and lashed out, the more outraged the people became.

'Off with his head!' they screamed furiously and repeatedly.

It was only when the executioner clambered up the steps did the shouting subside. With his head squeezed into a leather hood, and a deadly axe across his shoulder, he strode across the scaffold, creaking the timbers under his massive weight as he went. Coldly regarding the spectators with dark lifeless eyes, he set himself by the chopping block and rested his great gnarly hands on the axe handle.

As the crowd became boisterous again, the hunchbacked official shuffled forward, and began to read out the sentence loudly.

'Having lawfully been tried by His Majesty's Court and found guilty of robbery, arson, mayhem, kidnapping, larceny and grievous bodily harm, in defiance of all the King's laws, the accused prisoner, Ned Spoon, has been found guilty on all charges, and condemned to death. The sentence will now be carried out. May the lord have mercy on his soul.'

Still screaming and struggling violently, Ned Spoon was brought to his knees and his shaven head held over the chopping block. The executioner walked forward resolutely.

'Oh my gosh,' Sally wailed. 'It's going to happen. It's actually going to happen!'

Just as the executioner raised his axe, a tall sinewy man, his face hidden by lank greasy hair hanging to one side, ascended the scaffold. Most startling of all was his left eye shimmering in the afternoon light like a black star. He raised a hand. The executioner stopped mid-execution.

'It's him!' Inky gasped.

'Who? Where?' Sally cried, throwing a nervous glance towards the scaffold.

'Beside the executioner, it's Hemlock. I'd recognize that eye a mile off. Many a brave man has withered under that orb, I can tell you.'

A simmering murmur rumbled across the spectators as Hemlock held aloft a scroll fastened with a red seal.

'This is an official Court document, signed and delivered by the City Sheriff himself,' he roared – before carefully and ceremoniously handing the scroll to the executing official.

The official snapped open the seal and perused the contents. He glared at Hemlock, then the prisoner, and finally he gazed over the crowds.

'It would appear that the accused has been pardoned by the Court's mercy,' he gravely announced. 'Free the prisoner – he is no longer under sentence of death.'

The crowd booed in astonishment and anger. But it made no difference: Ned Spoon was a free man, and moments later he was handed over to Hemlock.

'And that's a perfect example of what infuriates

honest people,' said Herbert, biting his lip and shaking his head. 'The likes of Hemlock abusing the law any way he likes, while the rest of us obey.'

Disappointed and dejected the crowds began to disperse and leave Tyburn Hill. Toby was about to leave when a face caught his attention.

"I think I know that guy!" he thought, staring hard in the direction of the scaffold.

Toby craned his neck until he could clearly see the guard nodding and gazing up admiringly at Hemlock. It was him – the crazy soldier from London Bridge! The sight felt like a ton of bricks falling on Toby's head but moments later both Hemlock and the soldier were lost in the crowd.

'You ok, Toby?' Sally asked, noticing Toby frown.

'Yeah, everything's cool.' Toby answered calmly, deciding to keep his thoughts to himself. 'We should go now.'

On the way home it felt like all the enjoyment had been sucked out of London and replaced with gloom. The mood was made worse by a slow rain drizzling its way across the city. Later on, after too much lolling around and doing nothing much back at Puddle Street, Sally decided it was time to cheer things up.

'C'mon, you guys. I thought we were supposed to be enjoying ourselves. Did the world end when my back was turned. It's still only the afternoon. We have loads of time left on our day off.'

That seemed to trigger something in Inky. 'Hey! I've just remembered.' he said, slapping his forehead. 'Cockfighting!'

'Cockfighting?' Toby said doubtfully.

'Yes, at that new baiting arena near the Globe. There's a big match on this very evening – proper entertainment that.'

Sally burst out laughing.

'Are you bonkers, Inky? In what universe could a pair of chickens having a scrap be called entertainment. I mean, how gross can that be.'

'You haven't a clue,' Inky snapped, irritated by the scorn in Sally's voice. 'And tis cockfights… not blasted chicken-fights.'

'Whatever, have it your own way.' Sally shrugged and crossed her arms. 'But I think I'll pass if you don't mind.'

'Guh… as if,' Inky muttered, stomping away in a strop.

'And eh, see you later then, Sally.' Herbert muttered, awkwardly following after Inky.

Toby took a deep breath. 'Jeez Sal, sorry about that….'

'Sorry for what?' she laughed.

'You know, first the execution, and now this cockfighting thing….'

'Don't be silly, it's just not my scene, that's all.'

'So then… you won't mind if I go?'

'Toby, why would I mind? And even if I did, would you *not* go?'

'No I wouldn't ,' Toby squirmed winsomely. 'Although I might still *want* to.'

'Toby, just go. It's obviously what they do here for entertainment and I guess it's good to know what life is really like in these times. Anyway, a couple of hours on my own is exactly what I need. Just don't tell me the grisly details later.'

Sad-faced and apologetic, Inky stuck his head into the kitchen.

'Sorry for getting angry, Sally. I hope we're still

friends.'

'Everything's fine, Inky. We'll always be friends. I just don't like fighting of any description.'

'Aye – my mum agrees with you. She thinks fighting chickens are a waste of a roast dinner.'

And so it was, in the absence of the boys and for a short while at least, in the calming comfort of candlelight and a fragrant steamy bathroom, Sally enjoyed a simple good old-fashioned soak in the bath and forgot all about executions and cockfights and stupid broken-down time machines.

15. A TASTE OF HEMLOCK

Marshmallow-y clouds rolled across a purple sky, and a crescent moon rose from the east. It was the first time Toby had willingly separated from Sally since their mad adventure began. He felt anxious, lonely, and more than just a bit scared. But by the time they had stomped his way across a heavily packed London Bridge, with their eyes shining and faces reddened from the icy river breeze, he was starting to feel at ease.

Laughing and joking, the boys navigated their way along congested backstreets full of beggars, shouty people and barking dogs. Eventually they approached the dimly-lit arena, and it looked like London's entire male population was arriving at the same time. At about thirty feet in height with a thatched roof and painted brilliant white, the building resembled the Globe, at least on the outside. Inside was a very different story. A near-suffocating stench of filth, smoke and chicken poo hung cloud-like over the cramped circular fighting paddock. Torchlight flames danced around the walls adding extra layers of suspense to the already raucous atmosphere. Words almost failed Toby as he breathed in the putrid air.

'Ugggh,' he coughed, the stench stinging his lungs. 'How can you guys not smell that? It's like stink HQ in here.'

'Tis only chicken-muck,' said Herbert. 'Suck it in, lad – it's good for the tubes.'

'Let's grab those seats!' Inky shouted, steering them through the revelling throng.'

As soon as they were comfortably settled, Inky

elected himself as the official cockfighting expert. 'I got a great tip for a cock named *Killer Joe*,' he proclaimed with a sly nod. 'He's a sure thing, apparently!'

Toby and Herbert shot a questioning glance at each other.

'Yes.. I know. Gambling is never a great idea,' Inky continued. 'But I was thinking we might risk tuppence between us... maybe?'

'Oh alright. It's just a bit of fun I suppose.' Toby smiled.

With cash in hand, Inky was off, elbowing his way through the throngs towards the bookmaker stalls.

Herbert shrugged. 'That's tuppence we'll never see again.'

'It's worth it for a laugh.' Toby said, squinting through the smoky fug at a stack of cages with plumes of multicoloured feathers spiking-out through the bars.

In the middle of all the noise and clamour a tall flamboyantly dressed Master-of-Ceremonies made his grand entry into the fighting paddock. Raised fists, manly cheers and growling roars greeted his arrival.

'Good evening to one and all!' he bellowed. 'Welcome to another entertaining evening of sporting events on the banks of the beautiful river Thames.'

A riotous round of hooting, hollering, and booing pulsated through the stifling air.

'Gentlemen, gentlemen, please. I do understand some of you are in from the wilderness of Essex. However, you are in the genteel company of Southwark citizens this evening, and therefore you should at least try to behave in a civilized manner.'

Following that light-hearted slur, an avalanche of swearing, insults, and laughter poured into the fighting paddock.

'I can see I am wasting my time,' he went on. 'So I will dispense with decorum and get straight to tonight's stupendous extravaganzaaaaaa!'

Deafening cheers and hoots bounced around the arena walls as men jumped around with excitement. A bell chimed, a heavy door creaked open, and two trainers approached with cages under their arms. The hooting and cheering became impossibly loud.

'I am pleased to announce this evening's opening bout', the Master-of-Ceremonies yelled. 'Featuring that feathered warrior, the undefeated reigning champion, *Killer Joe,* and a new challenger, *Big Boy.'*

To riotous ovations the trainers carried their feathered warriors to the centre of the paddock. As was the norm, they began teasing and goading their little fighters into a squawking rage. As soon as the cockerel's fury had reached the required fever pitch they were released – whereupon *Killer Joe* ran away for the nearest exit.

'I don't believe it,' Inky cried. 'The chicken's done a runner!'

Toby laughed so loud he almost choked.

'Hey Inky,' said Herbert, flicking Inky's left ear. 'What do you think the odds were on that happening?'

Just then, over the booing and the laughing and the hissing, Inky's eyes widened with alarm. Hemlock and his cronies were approaching.

Moments later a rock-like finger jabbed into Toby's back.

'You...!' a voice growled. It sounded like it was coming from a deep dark hole. 'You're in Mr. Hemlock's seat. Move yourself while you still can.'

Flinching from the jabs, Toby spun round to face his assailant. He stiffened with shock. He was staring into the scarred face of that crazy Bloodnutt guy from London

Bridge.

'Well, runt. What are you waiting for?' Bloodnutt demanded, his rat-like eyes protruding out from his big reddening face. 'I said, move out.'

Maybe he was enjoying himself too much, or maybe he was just fed-up with being pushed around by people like Bloodnutt. Whatever the reason Toby gathered his courage, and smiled at the trooper.

'Actually, Frankenstein, we were here first. So, *you* shove off!'

Snorting with fury, Bloodnutt was about to launch a fist towards Toby's face – when he paused. His eyes narrowed into suspicious slits. He half-recognized Toby.

'No-no-no sir, my friend is mistaken.' Herbert blurted, while simultaneously dragging Toby from the seat. 'We were not here first. My friend is from up North you see... a-and doesn't understand the seating arrangements in London.'

Herbert's valiant attempt at defusing the situation wasn't working: Bloodnutt had suddenly remembered where he had seen Toby! He immediately re-launched his fist.

With hundreds of astonished gamblers looking on, Toby ducked beneath the incoming knuckle sandwich, which sent Bloodnutt spinning and flopping down onto his big fat behind. Inky and Herbert stared with open-mouths like they'd just witnessed some kind of insane joke. Thunderous outbursts of mocking laughter filled the arena. For the second time in a week Bloodnutt had been thwarted and made to look foolish by this runt. A happy bunny he was not. His mangled face turned the darkest possible shade of red.

Surveying this unfolding fiasco with disdain, Hemlock stepped forward. With a lightning fast move he produced a loaded pistol and pressed it to Toby's startled face.

'Leave this seat,' he said, with a sneery grin. 'Or leave this world.'

Toby could feel the hatred radiating from Hemlock. Swallowing hard, he stepped aside. As Hemlock moved forward to take his seat, small pockets of the crowd, hidden by the hazy smoke, hissed and jeered.

'Oh, there's one last thing,' Hemlock said out loud.

The arena froze. And before Toby realised what was happening, Hemlock's pistol had smashed across his face. Bloodnutt was about to join in the fray, but his superior raised a finger.

'There is a lesson here for you as well,' he said under his breath.

'Always keep a cool head, especially in front of enemies.'

With blood spilling from his nose, Herbert and Inky led a badly shaken Toby to safety. As soon as they were outside Inky confronted Toby.

'Here's a question,' he began, his mouth in a reflective pout. 'Before he lashed out, why did that madman look like he knew you?'

'Well, we do kind of know each other,' Toby mumbled, holding a hanky to his nose and his head back to stem the flow of blood.

'*Kind* of know each other?' Inky repeated – half laughing. 'Toby, you don't just *kind* of know a monster like that. You avoid them at all costs, and above all else you never start a fight with them. So, out with it, what's the real story?'

'There is no real story – it's like I said, we just kind of know each other. That's all.'

'Not a single word you just said is true. So I'll ask

again – and I'll keep on asking until you tell us. What is the real story?'

Toby took a deep unsteady breath.

'Ok, Ok, it's that mad soldier I told you about. Remember… at London Bridge?'

Inky and Herbert looked stupefied.

'Get off the stage!' Inky cried. 'We thought you were making it up. Or at the very least exaggerating just a tiny bit.'

'It's true, believe me. And there's something else, guys,' Toby continued unsteadily. 'I would prefer if Sally didn't hear about what just happened. She'd worry like crazy.'

'Huh, we won't have to say a word,' said Inky. 'Your nose will do all the talking.'

'Yeah well, let's just say I fell over and bashed my face, hence all the bruisey stuff?'

'Come off it, Toby.' Herbert said dismissively. 'Sally's no doctor, but even she'll recognise a walloped face when she sees one.'

'I don't care… the story is I fell over and bashed my head.' Toby tugged a strand of hair over the bruise. 'Fingers-crossed she'll never even notice. I need your promise on this, guys.'

Herbert shrugged.

'Fine, be it on your head.'

'Is that supposed to be a joke?'

'It is now.'

'I have to hand it to you, Toby,' said Inky. 'In less than a week you have managed to annoy two of the deadliest nutters in the city. Not bad going for a simple Northerner.'

Shifting uneasily Herbert glanced back over his shoulder.

'You know what, chaps – just in case Bloodnutt decides to reacquaint us with his fist again - maybe we should get as far away from here as possible.'

16. UNFORGETTABLE

With her chin propped into her cupped hands, and her elbows planted on the desk, Sally was pondering the big lie Toby and boys had told her this morning. Even with those strands of hair pulled across his forehead, no amount of smiling and fibbing could hide that bruise. Clearly Toby had been in a fight with someone and lost. But she wasn't too worried. She'd get the full story out of him eventually: she always did.

All of a sudden the office door swung open – and before she could think about Toby's bruises for another second, a well-dressed man was striding towards her with a hand extended.

'Miss Bunn. I am so pleased to meet you,' the man smiled. 'I'm told I must thank you for saving the Globe's bacon, so to speak. Therefore, thank you very much, my dear... we shall be forever in your debt! I'm Shakespeare. Burbage said you might expect me.'

Gasping with surprise, Sally sat rigid on the very edge of her seat. This was amazing. The great Bard himself was standing right there in front of her. And even though she tried her best to stay calm and normal looking: her face turned a bright scarlet and she started sweating profusely. All those old Shakespeare images from history books flashed through her mind. They weren't real photos of course, but at that very moment it was as if they had sprung to life. He looked almost exactly like them! And then there was the way he spoke. Her name seemed to curl from his mouth – Miss Bunn – big and clear and oh-so-nice.

Instead of responding in plain English: peculiar jibbering noises poured out of her mouth.

'Oh…h-hello… pleased to… you know… like, meet me… I-I-I mean meet *you* today…' she gulped and swallowed, struggling to get the words out, and immediately wishing she could suck them straight back in again.

'I have already met your cousin, Master Sprocket,' Shakespeare continued. 'He informs me you hail from up north. It is a part of the country I know well.'

Struggling to get her nervousness under control, Sally just about managed to say something half-normal.

'Bradford!' she blurted, the corners of her mouth twitching. 'We are from Bradford… that's like, in Yorkshire… you know, up in the north.'

Shakespeare's eyes widened. 'Yes, I do know Bradford is in Yorkshire,' he said with a slow nod. 'Regrettably it is a town I have seldom been to. Perhaps you might tell me about it sometime?'

'Yes. No. Sure. I mean…   we *could* do that… anytime… whenever, you know… name a day… a time even…'

Sally was not used to falling apart when she got embarrassed, and this was starting to get ridiculous. When it sounded like she might never stop saying the wrong things, Mr. Shakespeare kindly stepped in.

'I think you may have answered *yes* to us having a chat about Bradford'

Sally giggled. 'Sorry, Mr. Shakespeare. I'm usually not this uptight, I assure you. I'm just very nervous about meeting a famous person like you.'

'Well, we have met each other now, haven't we. So, we shall feel at ease in future. For the moment though, duty calls and I must depart. Again, let me thank you for all you have done for the Globe. I should also add that your family in... up in Bradford...? they must be very proud of you and Master Toby.'

'Oh, yes, I'm sure they are.' Sally whispered.

Before she could say anything else totally stupid, Mr. Shakespeare was already shaking her hand, saying farewell and departing the office.

For a full minute Sally just stood there, breathless and red-faced, her hand sticking out in front of her.

'Wow, wow, and wow! she thought. 'Did that just happen? Did that *really* just happen?'

17. CONSEQUENCES

It was late afternoon, and Hemlock was alone by a blazing fire watching smoke and sparks roaring up the chimney. A humourless grin pulled at the corner of his mouth as he recalled old battles and confrontations, and how his strength and cunning had always triumphed. He had never been defeated… ever. And he had no intention of being foiled now.

But something had changed. Out of nowhere an unfamiliar feeling was worming its way into his black heart. It was a feeling he had never experienced before – a feeling of doubt.

'I've been too soft!' he snarled, stabbing a cast-iron poker into flaming embers and pushing strands of oily hair from his forehead.

Jumping to his feet he prowled about his lair like a furious demon. Squeezing his hand into a white-knuckled fist he thumped the wall.

'Spoon!' he roared. 'Get in here.'

In a race to get to his master, Ned Spoon stumbled awkwardly into the room.

'You called, Boss!' he answered breathlessly.

Hemlock glared at his hapless lackey.

'I've reached a decision about the Globe,' he announced gravely.

'It shall be mine totally, or I shall destroy it totally.'

'Ahh, I'm glad to hear that, Boss,' Spoon sneered sweetly. 'You were too patient with that ungrateful lot down there, too patient by far.'

Hemlock poked at the fire again.

'Do you know what he had the impudence to ask me, Spoon?'

'W-Who, Boss?'

'That lying cheating swine, Shakespeare.' Hemlock hissed, bubbles of spit gathering at the corner of his mouth. 'He sat there, on that very chair, and calm as you like begged me to lower my fees. Begged me, he did. Ohhhh he was good... and I was this close, *this* close, to being taken in. And all the while Burbage was giving away pennies like there was no tomorrow. Three whole pennies, free, to every Tom, Dick, and Sprocket.'

'The swine, the absolute swine!' Spoon whinged agreeably.

'One thing I cannot abide, Spoon – is a liar and a cheat...   Ok, that's two things. There are *two* things I cannot abide, Spoon. Liars and cheats!'

'Aye, liars and cheats, Boss. The lot of them.'

'As you well know, Spoon. Being overly generous has always been a fault of mine. Well, not anymore. That *thrupenny* thing is the last straw. Squeezing the Globe for money is easy-peasy, and they pay-up every week without fail. They complain of course like everyone else. But unlike everyone else they are practically printing money.'

Spoon looked at Hemlock quizzically. 'Boss, why not just kill Burbage and Shakespeare and take over the place likes we usually do?'

'Because, you repulsive slug. Writers and actors are not bog-standard scum like you. They are not so easy to replace.'

'Ahhh, I see what you mean, Boss,' Spoon nodded slyly. 'Them actors are a strange bunch all right, and them writers are even stranger.'

'Needless to say when I *do* take control of the whole

shebang, and I have ownership of their plays and title deeds – top of the list will be getting rid of that annoying creature, Sprocket.'

'I know what you mean, boss. It's the talk of the town about how that how he trounced old Bloodnutt… twice!'

'Precisely!' Hemlock admitted. 'The wage monkeys are getting a bit too big for their boots. They need to be put back in their cages.'

Spoon rubbed his hands together. 'Now you're talking, Boss. That's what I call smart thinking.'

'Ok then,' Hemlock declared. 'I'm off to the Globe for a final little chat with Mr. Shakespeare. I'll show him it will take more than three pennies to grease my palm. You get the men ready for action later.'

'Aye sir---'

'…except for Dripping,' Hemlock mused, as he stroked his chin between thumb and forefinger. 'I'll take him with me. I haven't quite figured it out yet. But there's something queer about that lad…'

'Don't worry, boss. I'll keep the lads on their toes. How long will you be gone?'

'As long as it takes,' Hemlock replied, stomping out the door.

'Dripping!' Hemlock yelled.

'Yes, Master…'

'Follow me. We're going to the Globe!' Whereupon Sid trotted along after his master like a whipped puppy.

18. FIRED & HIRED

Outside the Globe, Toby nearly collided with Sid Dripping, who was busy chewing his fingernails and looking wretched. Ordinarily Toby would shout something rude at Hemlock's pet spy. But for some odd reason he felt sorry for him.

"Sup, Sid?' Toby said good-humouredly. 'You look like your head caught fire and Hemlock put it out with a shovel.'

'Piss off, Sprocket,' Sid snapped. 'I've no time for the likes of you today.'

Toby was on the verge of offering help. But Sid had already shot him an evil look.

'Ok. Have it your own way,' he chortled, raising a hand and walking on by.

As per usual Mr. S was up in the top gallery making edits to his play. Toby didn't want to disturb him but he did need to discuss the poster situation. He decided to take a chance, and as a peace offering he would bring along a mug of cool water.

Stealthily climbing the stairs, so as not to spill the water, he inched his way slowly along the top gallery. Just as he was about to say hello to Mr. S, he noticed a figure in the shadows.

He froze…

It was Hemlock, leaning against a pillar, his legs crossed at the ankles, calmly slicing a pear with a razor sharp knife.

'My patience is at an end,' he drawled, licking the pear juice that dribbled down his wrist. 'Therefore, I hope for the sake of all concerned ,you make the right decision. What, then, is your answer?

Shakespeare gulped. 'We have thought long and hard about your offer. But once again the answer is no,' he declared, slashing the air with his hand to show he meant business. 'We will continue our payments. But we cannot hand over our life's work willy-nilly. No sir, that we cannot do.'

'You say you cannot relent,' Hemlock replied sneeringly, sucking pieces of pear from his teeth. 'Yet Burbage *can*, apparently, hand over pennies to all-and-sundry. So I am afraid *no* is not an option.'

In a cold sweat, Toby looked back and forth between the two men. At that very moment a creaking board beneath his foot sounded like an explosion.

'And as for you, Master Sprocket,' Hemlock continued without a trace of surprise. 'You may think you are protected by the bogus shield of association. But you should inquire about what happened to a certain Mr. Marlowe when he crossed the wrong people.'

Hemlock glared down at Shakespeare with a mixture of fury and loathing. 'Your time has run out, writer!'

Like a snake preparing to strike, Hemlock hoisted himself over the cowering Shakespeare. A blade flashed. Instinctively Toby leapt forward, and for the second time in a week stepped into the unstoppable flow of history.

'HEEEEEEEEEELP!!!' he screeched until his throat almost caught fire. 'HELP, HELP, UP HERE…HEEEELP!'

Everybody at ground level instantly looked in the direction of the demented screeching. Hemlock leaned back into the shadows.

'Make no mistake, little boy,' he hissed through clenched teeth. 'You will pay for your interference this day. Indeed you will.'

In front of Toby's astonished eyes Hemlock seemed to dissolve into the shadows and vanish from sight. Meanwhile Mr. Shakespeare dropped his head into his hands.

'Thank you, dear boy. You saved my life,' he whispered. 'That monster was determined to kill me.'

'It's ok, Mr. S. He's gone now. We're both safe.'

Burbage charged up the stairs and stomped towards them.

'What in the name of Hades is going on here?' he bellowed.

'A great danger has passed,' a becalmed Shakespeare explained. 'And I'm happy to say that young Master Sprocket has saved me from deadly harm.'

'What do you mean, *deadly harm*. Explain yourself, Will?'

Taking a deep breath Shakespeare gave a blow-by-blow account of the terrifying event. Burbage looked profoundly saddened. He turned to Toby and bluntly announced. 'I am truly sorry to say this, lad. But you must leave the theatre, this instant.'

'Err… y-you lost me there, Mr. Burbage. Leave…?'

Burbage held up his hand. 'Please, Toby. I have no choice. You must leave us, today.'

'Wait – you're *firing* me. I don't understand?'

'Neither do I,' said Shakespeare, wrinkling his brow.

'Toby lad, the Globe cannot employ you now,' an embarrassed Burbage continued. 'That mangy dog Hemlock would make life damn near impossible if he heard you were still here after what's happened. I hope you understand, Toby. This is bigger than both of us. I have no other choice in the matter. I will, of course, give you a month's salary.'

Toby was devastated. Just as he was starting to enjoy his first ever job, he was being sacked.

'Eh, excuse me, Richard,' Shakespeare interrupted. 'I have an proposal that should keep everybody happy.'

'Which is…?'

'The lad shall work directly for me!'

'Work directly for you!' Burbage said confusedly. 'What do you mean?'

'Master Sprocket shall be my Personal Assistant,' explained Shakespeare. 'I shall pay his wages out of my own pocket thus freeing the theatre of any encumbrances. We must make sure this news reaches Hemlock's ear. Therefore he can then have no gripe with the Globe on the matter.'

Toby was both delighted and speechless. One moment he was fired and the next he was hired.

'Are you sure about this, Will?' Burbage asked, sitting beside Shakespeare.

'We'll hear no more about it,' Shakespeare insisted with a casual wave of a hand. 'It makes complete sense and will endanger no one but myself. And since I am already in danger, what difference will it make.'

'Mr. S, you really don't have to do this. I can look after myself.'

'Of that I am sure. You might even find your way back to York…. or is it Bradford?' Shakespeare said with a wink.

'I-I don't know what to say…'

'Toby. For reasons I do not fully understand, I believe your presence is of great consequence to me and to the Globe. You have already saved me from serious harm, which confirms that belief. And besides, I really do require a Personal Assistant.'

Toby scratched his head. It was obvious fate was not

finished messing with his life just yet. And this time he was entirely happy with that.

'Since you put that way, sir. I accept your kind offer.'

'Excellent,' Shakespeare said with a smile. 'Let that be an end to the matter. I should also say, you may take lodgings at my home on Silver Street if needs be.'

'Thanks a lot, Mr. S, but I think my friends need me around now more than ever. I really should stay in Puddle Street.'

'I do understand. There are times when friends must stand together. Nevertheless, my offer will remain open should you wish.'

Mr. Shakespeare looked hard at Burbage. A rumble of thunder approached the city.

A storm was brewing.

19. U-TURNS

Stretching claw-like fingers into black leather gloves, Hemlock's mood was beyond mere fury.

'You!' he growled, swirling around and pointing at Sid, who was still skulking by the Globe entrance.

'Yes sir – coming sir!' Sid wheedled, scampering over to his master.

Out of the blue, Hemlock smacked Sid so hard on the back of his head it almost sent him into the middle of last week.

'Owwwwww!' Sid howled, rubbing his throbbing head. 'What was that for?'

'Count yourself lucky that's all you're getting!'

'Lucky…?' Sid whimpered, his eyes blinking with pain and confusion.

Ignoring Sid, Hemlock railed on. 'Run ahead and tell Spoon to prepare my guest for a special interview. I'm in a suitable frame of mind for dealing with that particular little swine. Be quick about it, lad…' And to show he meant business, he gave Sid an extra hard kick up the backside.

'Owwwwwww!' Sid howled again, squirming in agony as he limped away in the direction of the docks.

Every day since Sid had joined Hemlock's gang, the sight of his dockside lair had sent shivers down his spine. The doom-laden walls leaning at peculiar angles, the slit windows like the squinting eyes of a beast. And most terrifying of all, the swarm of thugs slouching around the entrance like a flock of bored vultures.

That particular afternoon, as Sid approached the front

gate and saw who was standing there, his heart sank. It was the bear-like figure of Ned Spoon and that crazy guy from the Tower - Bloodnutt. His mind went to panic stations. Maybe he could sneak in through the back entrance? Or maybe he could just hang around outside until Hemlock appeared? It was too late... they'd seen him already. He would have to brave it out.

Marching boldly into the compound, Sid did his best to quell the terror in his voice.

'The boss wants you to have his guest ready, sir... I-I mean sirs!'

Ned Spoon hated everybody almost as much as Hemlock did. And right at that moment he especially hated the cringing little blimp grovelling in front of him. Much to Bloodnutt's amusement Spoon leaned down and glared contemptuously into Sid's petrified face.

'Dripping. I didn't think you could be more pathetic than you usually are. You remind me of a worm that needs a damn good squashing.'

Raking a hand through his greasy hair, Sid nodded. 'Yes sir, whatever you say, sir.'

'Repeat after me, Dripping. "I am a horrible disgusting worm that needs a damn good squashing!"'

Trembling, Sid did as ordered. 'I am a horrible disgusting worm that needs a damn good squashing, sir.'

'And do you know what we also do with horrible disgusting little worms?'

No sir... yes sir... I mean, I don't know sir?'

'We throw them to the dogs. Don't we, Mr. Bloodnutt?'

'Aye, that's right, Mr. Spoon – to the dogs they go!'

Desperate to appear less frightened, Sid laughed along with the other thugs: now gathering round for the fun. Sid's apparent lack of fear, however, only provoked

Spoon to be more vicious. Pinching Sid's nose with a pair of iron tongs seemed an appropriate response. Sid wailed in agony, and when the others took turns at kicking his already bruised backside – Sid was sure, for one horrifying moment, that this was the end for him.

'Please stop, Mr. Spoon, I'm begging you… the pain…. the pain!'

'Why should we stop,' laughed Spoon. 'The fun is only starting.'

And that was it for Sid.

Something snapped inside him.

The realization that his life was never going to get any better shocked him to the core. He'd had enough of these monsters, these demons, these heartless brutes. With every tear he cried that day he swore an oath to extract himself from their evil clutches and make amends for the trouble he had personally caused to some of Hemlock's victims.

Without warning, the entrance gates crashed open. Hemlock had returned. Everyone, including Spoon and Bloodnutt, backed away.

'What the hell is going on here?' he roared. 'I'm not paying you lot to jerk around all day!'

'No sir, we were just----'

'…. bring me that pathetic loser, Ponsonby.' Hemlock roared again, kicking a badly shaken Sid out of his way as he did so.

Moments later an abused and battered little man was dragged unceremoniously in front of Hemlock. Sid recognized him immediately – it was old Mr. Ponsonby, the shopkeeper from near the Globe.

'Says he can't pay, boss,' said Spoon. 'That's the third week in a row.'

Hemlock, slinked down beside the terrified

shopkeeper, pushed a sweaty coil of hair behind his ear, and stared into his bloodshot eyes.

'Ffff... I will never understand you, Ponsonby,' Hemlock said frowning, and throwing his hands in the air. 'I mean, why do you do this to yourself. Look what happens when you don't pay your dues.'

Hemlock looked up at Bloodnutt. 'I wonder why I bother sometimes. I really *do* wonder why I bother helping these people?'

'Y-You're right, Mr. Hemlock,' Ponsonby agonizingly agreed. 'It's my own stupid fault. The money will be here first thing tomorrow. I promise. I won't let you down. Tomorrow morning, first light, I will be here.'

'That's a wise decision,' said Hemlock, nodding with satisfaction. 'Don't you agree, Mr. Bloodnutt – that Ponsonby has made a wise decision?'

'I certainly do agree,' Bloodnutt said, deadpan and serious. 'A very wise decision.'

'Right so, off you go then,' Hemlock barked, cutting his prisoner free. 'Off you go back to your little shop.'

As soon as Ponsonby had staggered out of the building, Hemlock turned to his men.

'Tomorrow morning, I want a couple of you fine fellows to relieve Mr. Ponsonby of his money before he gets here. No broken bones, mind you. Just enough to get the job done.'

Although confused, Sid nodded and laughed along with the others.

'You look mystified, Dripping?' said Hemlock, noticing a flash of uncertainty on Sid's face

'No, no, no, sir. Everything is fine, just fine.'

'Come along, lad. Spit it out before I kick it out of you.'

'Well, sir, it's just... if old Ponsonby is bringing the

money here. Why go to the bother of taking it from him?'

To the sound of jeers and sneers, Hemlock looked scornfully at his befuddled minion.

'Dripping, Dripping, Dripping. Tomorrow, not only will we have our cash, Ponsonby will also remain in my debt. It is called repeat business.'

Even though Sid was already planning to warn Ponsonby, he guffawed and laughed along with the others until his face hurt.

And so it was, later that very night, a determined Sid Dripping crept silently along, hugging shadows and doorways until he reached Mr. Ponsonby's grocery shop.

'Please don't hurt me, Mr. Dripping,' a terrified Ponsonby begged as soon as he saw the little hoodlum. 'Mr. Hemlock promised I had until tomorrow morning.'

Sid took the old man's trembling hands into his own.

'Sir, you must listen to me. I am not here for your money. I am here to save your life.'

Ponsonby always assumed the worst in those who worked for Christian Hemlock. But such was the depth of emotion in Sid's voice, he decided to trust him.

'Right… ok…. I am listening,' he said quietly.

'There is a demon out to destroy you, sir,' Sid calmly continued. 'And his name is Hemlock. This very night, I advise you to take your family and get as far away from London as you possibly can.'

'I can't just pack-up and---'

'…do you want to live, Mr. Ponsonby?'

'O-Of course I want to live.'

'Then you must do exactly as I say. Hemlock intends to have you robbed tomorrow morning before you get to his den: you might even die in the process, he doesn't care either way. Because you, or someone else in your family, will continue to be in his debt, perhaps forever.'

From under his bushy eyebrows the old shopkeeper looked long and hard at Sid. 'I believe you,' he said solemnly. 'And I thank you from the bottom of my heart.'

Sid smiled consolingly. 'It's not all bad news. Someday Hemlock will be gone. Then, and only then, can you return to start your life over again.'

And that was that...

The die was cast...

Sid's dangerous plan of redemption was up and running.

In the following days Sid played a dangerous game of appearing to enjoy the gang's brutality whilst at the same time warning potential victims. He hoped no one in the gang noticed his change of heart, at least not until his mission was complete.

His deception couldn't last forever. He knew that. And it wasn't long before Hemlock noticed the shortage of victims and money. One dark stormy night he summoned the gang together.

'I bring you here on this cold night to give you some terrible news,' he announced, his pallid face quivering with rage. 'A traitor has infected our jolly clan.... yes, that's what I said, a dirty traitor. But worry not: for I shall unmask that double-crossing dog quick enough. And trust me, when I do, I will burn him and bash him and stamp him into the ground. No one evades my revenge for long.'

His gaze moved from one terrified face to another. He wanted his message to swell inside their hearts.

'To prove I mean business, every man jack of you will be interrogated by our friend and colleague, Mr. Bloodnutt,' he nodded towards the Tower guard by his elbow. 'You all know his talent for squeezing answers out the hardest of nuts, and that is exactly what awaits you. Naturally, all that bother can be avoided if the traitor owns-up and admits his guilt.'

His cold black eye scanned the sea of frightened faces for any takers. Sid crept in behind the biggest slob he could find.

'Oh God, maybe he already knows...' he thought. *'...and he's just toying with me?'*

Hemlock lifted his chin and shrugged. 'Fine, if that's the way you want to play it. Interrogations will start in five minutes. Brace yourselves.'

Ned Spoon prowled around like an irritated demon. 'This is no practice drill, boys. Someone's been squealing and we're all gonna pay for it.'

The gang members' shrieks of terror could be heard spilling into the night when Bloodnutt commenced his dirty work. Sid was grief-stricken and riddled with guilt. But, much like the others, he knew there was no way out. A sudden thump on his back nearly knocked him over.

'Your turn, Dripping,' Spoon ordered, a malicious grin cutting across his face. 'Try not to scream too loud.'

As soon as Sid was flung into a darkened room, steely hands grabbed him by the scruff of his neck. Fully expecting the onset of torment and pain, he was utterly confused when instead he was simply pushed onto a chair.

'Old man Ponsonby,' Hemlock' voice began, as he appeared out of the shadows like a two-legged snake. 'Remember him, Sid? The grocer who cheated me out of my money.'

Sid did his best to sound calm. 'Pon-son-by.... yes, sir. I do remember that name?'

'Funny thing is, Sid. The morning after my little chat with him, he up'd and disappeared. Vamoosed right out of the city. What do you think about that, Sid?'

Sid scratched his head in confusion. 'It sounds odd, sir. Very odd.'

'Indeed it does, Sid. It's almost like he was *warned*.'

Sid swallowed. '*Warned*? Surely not, sir!'

Scrutinizing Sid's increasing nervousness, Hemlock turned the screw. 'Oh, but surely yes, Sid. As a matter of fact we know for certain it was somebody from our own ranks who warned him, plus lots of other clients.'

'What's the matter, runt...' Bloodnut roared into Sid's face, his breath smelling like a bag of dead fish. 'You look like you lost a pound and found a bent penny.'

'I'm sorry, Mr. Bloodnutt,' Sid sniffled, his entire body trembling and sweating. 'I don't know about bent pennies or any other kind of pennies. And I don't know why you're asking me about this. You can't possibly think I would ever betray Master Hemlock.... I-I swear to you... I never would....'

Like a giant spider slithering down his silky web, Hemlock dropped an inch from Sid's petrified face.

'My dear little maggot,' Hemlock purred, sliding an arm around Sid's trembling shoulder. 'Do you imagine for one second we would be having this little tête-à-tête if I thought you were a traitor. As you well know, my lad: Hell hath no fury like a Hemlock stabbed in the back. No, no, Sid. I look upon you more as a human foot-stool than a filthy spy.'

'Thank you, sir. That's exactly what I am... a-a human foot-stool.'

'But... guess what, Sid. Even someone like you can earn a chance to be trusted sometimes.'

'Really, sir?'

'Yes, Sid, really. And as it happens, I require a chap who can be trusted. A new chap who won't pull a vanishing act if the going gets tough. Would you like to be that new chap, Sid?

Sid was overjoyed by this lucky turn of events. He grabbed the chance with both hands.

'Yessir, yessir, of course I would. Whatever you need doing, sir – I'm your man.'

'That's the right attitude, Sid. Because you see, for the next 24 hours I will need a chap to keep a special eye on Mr. Shakespeare. Follow him everywhere. Do not let him out of your sight. And if you notice anything the least bit suspicious, no matter how trivial, I want to know about it.'

'Of course, Sir, but---' Sid's voice dropped to a whisper. 'Am I allowed to inquire why?'

There was no turning back now. Sid had manoeuvred himself to either the brink of success or the brink of disaster. Gritting his teeth, he tried his best to look especially keen and evil.

'I only ask because I can tell this mission is really important,' he continued. 'And I *so* want to do a good job.'

Hemlock stood back, folded his arms, and for a few scarifying moments, stared coldly at Sid. He exchanged a sharp look with Bloodnutt. The Tower guard nodded slowly. The blazing tension left the room.

'Well then, Dripping,' Hemlock nodded slowly. 'You better listen up, then.'

Sid opened his mouth to say something, but the words stuck in his throat. Fear gnawed at him, and the very air purred with malice.

'Most evenings,' Hemlock continued. 'Between the hours of six and eight o'clock. Mr. Shakespeare takes time out to work alone at Silver Street. Tomorrow evening will be different. Very different. I intend to relieve him of his plays, the deeds to the Globe, everything he owns in fact – and then I will relieve him of his life. A job like that requires perfect timing. And that's where you come in.'

Hemlock moved to the centre of the room. 'Don't look so worried, lad,' he grinned. 'I don't expect *you* to do it. All you have to do is knock at his door and look all honest and virtuous. You see, he never opens his door without checking through the spyhole first. And since he knows you, and when you say you have a special message from me, he will open the door.'

Like a mist in a storm, Hemlock's grin evaporated.

'As soon as that door is open, we take over.'

While keeping an eye fixed on Sid, Hemlock leaned towards Bloodnutt. 'And I'm sure the arrangements for his family in Stratford are in place?'

'Don't worry, Boss,' said Bloodnutt. 'That particular target will be taken care of at exactly the same time. The message will not be lost on anyone.'

The terrible reality of what Sid was hearing exploded inside his head. They were planning to kill innocent people, and *he* was to play a big part in it.

Reaching into his pocket, Hemlock approached his special new spy. Instinctively Sid pulled his arms over his head.

'Calm yourself, lad,' Hemlock laughed, pulling out two pennies and dropping them into Sid's top pocket. 'This is your big opportunity, Sid. Your time to rise above the rabble. Do not let me down.'

A scared little voice in Sid's head said, *Because if I do, I'll be dead meat.*

Sid would remember that day and those scenes forever: Bloodnutt's sweaty face, the look of hatred in the eyes of Spoon and the others, and the sheer relief at leaving that awful place in one piece.

It felt like his brain had been smeared with evil and wickedness. And try as he might he could not shake off the suspicion that it was all just an elaborate set-up to ensnare him. Deep down though, he knew it wasn't. It was real. Before his luck and his courage ran out he had a vitally important message to deliver.

He started running towards Silver Street.

20. A RISKY RENDEZVOUS

Toby, Sally and the boys were busy tucking into the latest super delicious *Mutton Stew à la Blyster,* when a loud knock-knock-knocking rattled the front door. Rushing out to answer, Sally found an urchin standing there with a face like a frightened fish.

'Yes – can I help you?' she said with a smile.

'Is there a Sprocket here?' The urchin nervously inquired, straining his neck to see around Sally.

'I'm a Sprocket,' said Toby, arriving. 'What's up, kid?'

The urchin shoved a sealed note into Toby's hand.

'From Mr. S,' he whispered conspiratorially, and then promptly disappeared into the night.

'Wonder what this is all about?' said Toby, unfolding the note. The others crowded around him.

'It's Mr. S all right. He wants to meet us at The George Inn, of all places. "Please be quick" he says, "and be careful you are not followed."

'Gadzooks!' Herbert exclaimed. "Be careful you are not followed!" What do you think that means?'

'It means what it says,' said Toby. 'And it sounds like we should leave straightaway.'

Following a quick shufti along the street to check for suspicious looking characters, they prepared to make a dash for it.

'Hold it, guys,' Toby said dramatically. 'I was thinking – in case we *are* followed, maybe we should split-up?'

'Makes sense,' said Inky. 'You and Herbert should go

that way, and Sally and I will go this way.'

A speedy succession of running, ducking and hiding followed until they arrived, almost together, at the George Inn. It was a rambling higgledy-piggledy building with three terraced floors and a partially open roof. Groups of drinking men were sitting around a big open fire and a long serving counter. Away in a quiet corner, in the glimmer of the fire, a figure sat huddled by a table.

'That's Mr. S there,' said Inky, nodding towards the figure.

Apprehensively crossing and re-crossing his legs, Mr. S visibly relaxed at the sight of his young friends.

'Herbert and Inky. Might you stand watch outside for any sign of Hemlock's men?' Shakespeare asked with a fearful expression. 'And if you do see anything irregular: tap twice on the window – the one here behind me – and then get away as quickly as possible.'

'No problem, sir.' Inky said determinedly, heading back outside with Herbert.

Toby could hear the edge in Shakespeare's voice.

'Ok, Mr. S,' he said quietly. 'What's going on?'

Gulping down a mouthful of ale, Mr. Shakespeare made a startling announcement.

'Time is of the essence so I'll get straight to the point. After our recent deadly exchange with Hemlock, Burbage and I came to the conclusion that we could no longer guarantee workers' safety at the Globe. And therefore, with great reluctance, we have decided to relent and give-in to Hemlock's demands. We had even agreed a meeting for the hand-over, when something very strange happened.'

'Something strange?' Sally queried, already shocked at what she was hearing.

'It happened this very afternoon as I was making my way home. A young lad appeared out of nowhere, and I have to say I was less than welcoming when I saw it was one of Hemlock's mob.'

'"Please sir – wait – " the lad half-whispered, trotting alongside me and tugging my sleeve."'

'"Why should I wait for the likes of you?" I said, just wanting to be rid of him.'

'"Because I can do something for you, sir." He replied.'

'"*You* can do something for *me*?"'

'"Aye, and for your family!"'

'"My family! What are you blathering about, lad?"'

'"Mr. Shakespeare. If you go to your house on Silver Street this day, you will be attacked and most likely killed. Instead you must go straight to Stratford and protect your family. I say this because I believe they are also in mortal danger."'

'"If this is your idea of a joke?" I said. "You are a very sick individual."'

'"Sir, you must listen to me. Hemlock has decided that the Globe and all the people connected with it, have embarrassed him once too often. It's bad for business and bad for his image, he says. Therefore, he intends to violently remove you and take possession. It will look good to do it that way, he says. In fact, he is lying in wait, expecting *me* to spring his deadly trap. If you come along, I will prove it to you."'

'Cautiously the lad led me towards a shady corner at the far end of Silver Street. "Keep your head down," he whispered as we crept forward.'

'We stayed hidden for less than a minute, until we heard the faint sound of footsteps.'

'"Now…there…look…"' he whispered and pointed.

'And lo and behold, ducking down behind a wall opposite my house, I saw Hemlock and a bunch of his thugs, armed to the teeth.'

'Oh my God!' I thought, 'It is true then! He is waiting to kill me. What am I to do?'

'"First you need to get away from here," said the lad, grabbing me by the wrist and pulling me along. "You must get to Stratford as quickly as possible. You should also arm yourself. A terrible danger is heading towards your family, I am sure of it."'

'As you can imagine I was badly shaken by these events and I heartily thanked the lad and implored him to leave Hemlock's gang. I even offered him refuge.'

'"Nuh-uh, sir." He replied. "I thank you. But it's best I re-join Hemlock and convince him that you somehow managed to evade my surveillance and then vanished. If I don't, he will know something is amiss, and lord knows what might happen then."'

'With that, the lad dashed away to re-join his master.'

Sally blinked in amazement. 'This young chap. You obviously know him?'

'Oh, I'm sorry, did I not tell you? It was none other than young Dripping.'

'Sid Dripping!' gasped Toby and Sally together, the very idea jolting them upright.

'I truly believe where darkness reigned, clarity now leads this brave young chap. I am also deeply concerned for his safety.'

'Ok, you've convinced us,' said Toby. 'We'll deal with the Sid thing later. What do you want to do right now?'

There was no mistaking the relief on Mr. Shakespeare's face. There was also no mistaking his feelings of guilt. Enlisting the help of innocent young people, no matter how enthusiastic they might be, played heavily on his conscience.

'In all honesty, I should not be placing you in such danger. As a responsible adult I should instead be advising you to go home and forget all about this.'

'Mr. S. Don't go stressing yourself about events you have no control over,' said Toby. 'Besides, we were already in a heap of trouble before we met you. Also, doesn't Hemlock have a grudge against all of us?'

'Yes he does.'

Sally put a comforting hand on Mr. Shakespeare's shoulder.

'So he will try to harm us no matter what we do.'

Mr. Shakespeare took a deep breath and smiled.

'That is true. So then… Are you still willing?'

'Still willing? Of course we are!' Toby said and Sally nodded in agreement.

Grabbing a quick look around the packed Inn, Shakespeare reached down and dragged out a small wooden casket from under his seat. He placed it on his knees.

'This contains all my manuscripts and personal documents. My task for you, Toby, is to keep it safe in Puddle Street until I return from Stratford.'

'As good as done!' Toby answered assuredly.

'I have a small task for you too, Sally. The final draft and notes for *Winter's Tale* are in the office strongbox. I believe you hold a key? Masters Herring and Blyster might accompany you to collect them?'

'Also as good as done,' Sally said confidently. 'So – just go!'

'Thank you my friends…. you have no idea how much this means to me.'

With that, he pulled his cape tightly about his

shoulders and departed vigilantly through a back door.

'Phew,' Sally said at last. 'That was some meeting.'

'You can say that again!' Toby sighed. 'and I suppose we should give the boys the good news about Sid.'

Outside in the darkness, Inky and Herbert were overjoyed.

'Sid! You mean *our* Sid?' Inky repeated as if hearing things.

'Yesiree… that's him back in the gang and no mistake.' said Herbert.

'We'll soon have him sorted out.' Inky declared as if Sid's immediate return was a sure-fired certainty.

'I think we need to calm down, guys. First I have to get this chest back to Puddle Street, while you and Sally collect those documents from the Globe.'

Moments later the four friends eagerly set about their tasks. And as soon as Toby reached Puddle Street, he was up to the attic in a flash. Loosening-up some floorboards next to the Mark 5, he carefully hid the chest away, and hammered the boards back in place.

'There, done and dusted,' he said gladly. 'Here's hoping things work out as easy at the Globe.'

21. AMBUSH

A rusty hinge screamed like a banshee when Inky pushed through a rarely used side-door of the Globe. Once she reached her office, Sally fumbled around in the half-light for the strongbox key.

'There, found it,' she said at last, unlocking the box and extracted the documents. 'Ok. Let's get ourselves home.'

Just as they pulled the screeching door closed again, they almost died of fright when Hemlock and a squad of heavies loomed out of the darkness.

'Good evening, maggots!' Hemlock beamed an evil smile. 'I wonder what has dragged you out at such a late hour. Could it be what you have in your hand, Miss Bunn?'

Hemlock yanked the script from Sally's grasp and held it up to the light of a waning moon.

'Well, well, well... it seems coming here was a good idea after all, Mr. Spoon.'

'It's like I said, Boss, they're all in it together!' Spoon sniggered gleefully.

'That is patently true, I fear. But I'm putting a stop to all that right now.'

With lightning speed Hemlock grabbed Herbert by the throat and pinned him to a wall.

'Where is Shakespeare? Tell me, and I might let you live.'

'I-I don't know what you're talking about?' Herbert croaked.

A gloved hand smashed across Herbert's mouth

sending him crashing to the ground. In the same instant Hemlock's attention switched to Sally. He seized her roughly by the hair.

'Leave her be, creep!' Inky shouted, before he too was thumped to the ground.

Hemlock hesitated. A deadly tactic was hatching in his head. Shooting a strange look at Sid, he pulled out a knife and held the blade an inch from Sally's eye.

'Blyster. You have one second before I cut her eye out. Where is Sh---'

'....He's-with-Toby-in-Puddle-Street,' Inky blurted.

The gangsters burst out laughing at Inky's lovesick exhibition.

'Ok, here's what's going to happen,' Hemlock sternly announced. 'You two will inform the brave Mr. Shakespeare that he has two hours to get back here with everything I want. Or else....' He pulled Sally roughly to his side. '...The wench dies. Do I make myself clear, boys?'

'Yes sir, absolutely clear!' Herbert replied, his trembling fingers touching his bloodied lip.

'Good... good,' Hemlock nodded grimly. 'However, I think it is important the writer knows I mean business.'

With a nod from Hemlock, his thugs pounced on Inky and Herbert like a pride of hungry lions pouncing on a pair of antelopes. They immediately began beating the boys with fists and cudgels. They fought back bravely, but this only spurred-on their attackers to strike even harder. Fearing the worst, Sid sprang forward.

'Please, Mr. Hemlock. Make them stop,' he begged. 'They've had enough. They will do as they're told now, I know they will. Just stop... please!'

Sid's intervention did bring an end to the beating, but it wasn't the end of the brutality. Looking up at the night sky, Hemlock bared his pointed teeth as if remembering something dreadful.

'Thank you, boy. That is all I needed to hear. Now I know for certain who the traitor is. It is you, Dripping. YOU!'

'Sir, I swear--'

'...You swear what? That you just happened to bump into Mr. Shakespeare in the street this afternoon, and you just said hello?'

Poor Sid, knowing he was in deep trouble, could feel the blood draining from face.

'That's right, Dripping, I had you followed. You went behind enemy lines and I had you followed.'

'B-But sir, I was simply doing what you told me to,' Sid stammered, struggling to sound believable. 'And then---'

'...No Sid, you weren't *simply* doing anything I told you to do.' Hemlock cut in with a wagging finger. 'You were actually making the biggest mistake of your miserable little life. Do you take me for a complete fool? Have I got "idiot" stamped on my forehead? I made you my 'personal little spy' to confirm what I already suspected. So come along now, out with the truth and save your friends from paying a very heavy price.'

A jangle of knife blades flashed and held to the throats of Sally, Herbert, and Inky.

'Ok, ok, I admit it,' Sid cried, snot and tears streaming down his face. 'I did warn Shakespeare. I just couldn't live with another death on my conscience. But I'm begging you sir, please don't hurt my friends. I'll do anything you say, sir. Anything.'

Hemlock's dark eye gleamed with cold satisfaction. He took Sid's chin between his thumb and forefinger and raised his weeping face towards his.

'Well now, my filthy little traitor,' said Hemlock, his voice dropping to a low growl. 'You are in a fine pickle and no mistake. But since you have freely volunteered to atone for your treachery, there is one thing you can do.'

'Anything you say,' Sid blubbered, when a tiny glimmer of hope was dangled in front of him. 'Just name it, sir. Just name it.'

Hemlock whipped out a pistol, pressed it to Sid's chest, and whispered into his ear.

'You can die for me.'

A shot echoed down the empty streets like rolling thunder. Sally screamed at the top of her voice, as Sid fell to the ground like an empty sack.

Hemlock turned to the shocked faces of Inky and Herbert.

'Now. Go deliver my message,' he ordered with a dismissive wave of his hand. 'And remember...two hours or she joins the late Master Dripping.'

A monstrous act had been carried-out in front of Inky and Herbert's disbelieving eyes. And before they could even begin to come to terms with that, they had to listen to Sally's sorrowful cries as she was dragged away into the night.

22. TRAPPED

Fuzzy, broken images swam through Sally's mind. Worst of all was the sight of Sid's lifeless body on the cold ground. Words could not describe her sadness.

All at once she sensed a presence staring down at her. Without opening her eyes she knew it was Hemlock. A scream threatened to leap from her mouth: her lips opened, but somehow she managed to stop it. Gulping back sobs of terror she dug her fingernails into her palms and went completely rigid. Very quickly, she realised she was tied-up on a blanket that stank of sick and wee. The smell was so awful it made her head spin.

Convinced she was successfully carrying-off her pretend coma, the knot of dread relaxed in her stomach.

A minute passed.

'Ah good, you are awake,' Hemlock said, his voice jarring. 'I was beginning to get worried.'

Sally flinched, but remained totally still.

'It's no use faking, my dear. I know you can hear me. Perhaps one of my boys should give you a little shake? That might clear the sleep from your pretty little head.'

Such an alarming suggestion was enough for Sally.

'No-no sir, that won't be necessary,' she sighed, releasing her captured breath. 'I am awake now.'

From the corner of her eye she could see a huge tallow candle casting a flickering light, and Hemlock sitting in a tatty leather chair reading Mr. Shakespeare's play. Every so often he shook his head, stifled a guffaw, and then turned another page.

Because her bindings were so tight, hot rivulets of

pain shot through her body. She gritted her teeth, but the pain got worse and worse.

'Please, Mr. Hemlock,' she groaned, her voice shaking. 'Could you possibly loosen these ropes…. it is unbearable.'

Paying no attention, Hemlock continued his reading.

'Please Mr. Hemlock, sir,' Sally continued weakly. 'I really can't bear it.'

Hemlock stared blankly at the whimpering girl. Finally he nodded, and immediately a hulking henchman trundled across the room. He was so immensely fat the entire floor juddered with each plodding step. A knife blade flashed. Sally flinched again. Her bindings flew open with a tight snapping sound. The relief was instant and blissful.

'Thank you,' she said softly, massaging her aching wrists and hands.

In an effort to get her bearings – and to check for possible escape routes – she sat up to scan her surroundings. She was in a low musty-smelling room with a small circular window partially hidden by a mesh of raggedy curtains. Mildew-covered walls were festooned with all kinds of nasty weapons, heavy manacles and rusty chains. A thick wooden door studded with nails like iron warts was the only exit. Unfortunately, stationed by the door was that hulking henchman leering in Sally's direction. And that was it. Escape was not an option.

'I have a question,' Hemlock asked as if starting a friendly conversation. 'This play or whatever it is called. I believe it to be utter rubbish. What say you?'

Sally thought carefully before giving what she hoped was a safe answer.

'Umm… well, it is said Mr. Shakespeare's work is

very good, amazingly good in fact.'

'Yes, yes, yes, that's all fine and dandy. But you,' Hemlock persisted. 'What do *you* think?'

Sally raised an eyebrow. 'Actually, I also think his work is amazing and will last forever.'

Hemlock looked sideways at her.

'Hogwash,' he pshawed. 'The only thing that lasts forever is death, a fact that you will see for the second time this very night.'

Sally stared at Hemlock. 'What do you mean by that? Isn't controlling the Globe enough for you?'

'Huh... the Globe. Hardly, my dear. That grubby building means little to me. I could snap my fingers and have it destroyed this second.'

'So, why are you doing this?'

'The answer to that is simple,' Hemlock answered dryly. 'I have my men everywhere: in the Tower, the army, all the great halls of our city. In other words, I hold a position of strength and power. It has taken me many years to arrange this and keep it secure. Accordingly, to maintain my standing, I cannot allow resistance to my will. Every so often lessons need to be taught.'

He shot a dark look at Sally.

'And first up for a lesson will be Shakespeare and Burbage. They pretend they cannot afford to pay for my protection services, and yet they can easily afford to pay extra money to their little wage monkeys? Also by resisting my kind offer to run the Globe for them, has made me look – in the eyes of my enemies – not particularly strong *or* powerful. These situations have sent out all the wrong signals. Therefore I intend to stamp it out... permanently.'

Sally's mouth fell open. Was it her fault that this monster was going bat-shit crazy? Could finding that money have been such a bad thing? It would be a waste of time trying to explain to Hemlock where that money came from. So she decided to say nothing. It was also at that moment that she realised, regardless of what might happen at the Globe, that Hemlock had no intention of releasing her.

'You shouldn't fret, my dear,' Hemlock continued disdainfully. 'Shakespeare suffers from the same weakness you do – pointless compassion. That's why I am sure he'll be popping along to the Globe, as I demanded.'

An abrupt hammering at the door made Sally jump. The fat henchman yanked it open.

'The men are ready, boss,' a voice shouted.

Jumping up, Hemlock pulled Sally to her feet.

'The time for talking has passed. I am about to put an end to all this trouble-making. We'll be moving fast, so unfortunately, a rope around your slender neck will be necessary. And I'm giving you fair warning, any tricks and you will suffer greatly.'

With frost twinkling like silvery sand and a mist so thick it felt almost solid, a company of ripply shadows trotted their way along the banks of the Thames. All Sally could see in front of her was the rope disappearing into a wall of fog. Every-so-often she fell to the ground only to be dragged along yelling in pain.

'Hells bells,' Hemlock hissed. 'One more squeak out of you and I'll fill your mouth with rags.'

'I am sorry, Mr. Hemlock,' Sally whimpered, shrinking beneath his savage stare. 'I'll be extra quiet, I-I promise.'

Before too long they came to a halt, and the only sound to be heard was the gasping and spluttering of tired-out gangsters.

Sally, panting and sweating, looked anxiously around.

They had arrived at the Globe.

23. RUNNING THE NIGHT

Sid was dead.

Actually dead.

Choking with grief, Inky fell to the ground beside his old friend, weeping uncontrollably.

'Look at what that monster has done, Herbert. Just look at what he's done.'

While Herbert was just as distressed by the loss of Sid – uppermost in his mind was the fate of Sally.

'Inky, we really need to get going,' he whispered gently. 'The pain is over for poor old Sid. And he wouldn't want Sally to suffer. He would want us to help her as best we can.'

'Yes, of course, you're right,' said Inky, straightening up.

'We need to concentrate on Sally. We also have to tell Toby. Although I have no idea how we're going to do that.'

At the very moment they were turning to leave an unexpected sound brought Inky to a stop.

'What was that?' he cried, cocking his head. 'There… again… listen!'

Inky looked down at Sid. His heart jolted.

'Herbert… I think he's alive? Sid is alive!'

Dropping to his knees, Inky gently raised Sid's head.

'Come along old friend, don't you worry. We'll look after you now. We'll make you better.'

He pulled Sid's shirt open. 'Holy Moses! You are not going to believe this, Herbert?'

'What?'

'That big stupid knife of his. It deflected the shot. Look!'

Although it had shattered a rib or two on the way, the shot had indeed been deflected by the knife, without touching a single vital organ. In fact, all Sid would require was a few stitches and lots of rest.

'Must...help...Sally...' Sid groaned, slipping in and out of consciousness.

'Yes, yes, of course we'll help Sally.' Herbert promised, as he and Inky balanced Sid between their shoulders. 'But first we need to get you home.'

As soon as Toby saw the boy's staggered approach, he knew something was seriously amiss. Rushing onto the street he was shocked to find Sid being carried between the boys.

'What's wrong... what happened? And where's Sally?'

'Toby, there's no easy way of telling you this, so we're just going to say it.'

The boys calmly related the terrible events of the last hour or so. For a few moments Toby just stood there, rooted to the spot, his head spinning in a million different directions. He was only stirred to action by the thought of what Hemlock was capable of.

'Guys, we need to get going now. We've got to save her.'

'Toby, it's not as simple as that,' Inky corrected him. 'For one thing we have no idea where he's holding her?'

'And eh... guys,' Herbert grimaced, battling to keep Sid on his feet. 'We'll need to get Sid sorted.'

Only then did Toby realize the pitiful state Sid was in. 'Oh yes... let's get him inside.'

Not long after, with his wounds cleaned and bandaged, a semi-conscious Sid was resting on the sittingroom couch.

'At least the bleeding has stopped,' said Herbert. 'I think the worst is over.'

Sally's deadly predicament was swirling around Toby's head. The impossible distance from everything he loved and the fear of being stuck here forever had been terrifying – and now there was this heart-breaking event to deal with. For the first time since their adventure began he felt utterly defeated and lost.

'Surely the plays and documents will buy her freedom?' he thought out loud. 'I mean it's worth trying, isn't it? *Anything* is worth trying. And Mr. S will understand, I'm sure he will.'

A feeble voice spoke: it was Sid, dragging himself upright.

'Toby, listen to me. You must forget all about trying to appease Hemlock. He doesn't want to do a deal now. It's a waste of time.'

'What? You can't know that for sure. Hemlock said he wanted the plays and documents didn't he? Well, I can deliver all of it to him right now, this very night.'

Swallowing with difficulty, Sid spoke again. 'Toby, you're still not listening. One way or another, Hemlock intends making an example of you all. Yes, he will gladly take what you bring, smile and maybe even thank you. But then he will kill you. Besides any of that, he doesn't want to see you or me or anybody else. He only wants Shakespeare and Burbage, essentially so he can kill them. Then and *only* then will the city know who is back in charge. Believe me, Toby – the only thing you should be thinking about now is how to rescue Sally. That's *rescue,* Toby. No deals, no talking, just rescue.'

The effort proved too much for Sid. He coughed, on the verge of passing out again.

'Never... trust... Hemlock...' he croaked, as Inky grabbed him mid-faint.

Scowling with frustration Toby felt an overpowering desire to hit back at Hemlock.

'If only I could get my hands on some proper weapons,' he said, half mumbling. 'Like a tank or a flame-thrower. Then he'd know what's what.

Inky placed a steadying hand on Toby's shoulder.

'Toby, Sid is right. What we need is to come-up with a realistic rescue plan.'

'Aye,' Herbert agreed. 'And since Mr. S is halfway to Stratford, the best man to help us is Burbage. He knows Hemlock as well as anyone.'

'Well then, let's get over there,' Toby pressed.

As soon as they had made Sid as comfortable as possible, the three lads ran out the door.

They charged blindly along, panting and gasping, until finally, on reaching Burbage's house, the pounded on the front door. A small hatch flipped open and the barrel of a blunderbuss poked out.

'If that's you, Hemlock. You can go to blazes!' Burbage shouted.

'We've changed our minds! We won't be giving you anything. So if you don't want a mouthful of this, you better get going---'

'.... please open up, Mr. Burbage. It's us!' Herbert interrupted, pushing his face up to the hatch.

'Herring! What in heavens name are you doing here?'

'Hemlock has kidnapped Sally and we desperately need your help!'

'Oh my word! Come in, come in,' Burbage muttered, tugging at a string of locks and bolts.

Scrambling inside, the boys swiftly explained the awful situation. And although Burbage listened quietly and calmly, his anger was rising like a kettle slowly coming to the boil.

'By Jove, this is intolerable,' he thundered. 'We have suffered at the hands of this scoundrel for long enough. I say it is time to make a stand. And we shall start by getting the word out!'

'G-Getting the word out.' Toby stammered. 'I'm not sure how that will help---'

'...Toby lad,' Burbage calmly interrupted. 'The only way to save Sally is by defeating Hemlock. He's expecting to meet Shakespeare at the Globe in approximately ninety minutes. Well then, I shall muster a battalion of brave willing men and give the charming Mr. Hemlock a meeting he won't forget in a hurry.'

Toby scratched his head. 'But Mr. Burbage. How can we organize something like that on such short notice?'

'It is only a matter of geography and time, Toby. We must start immediately and get the word around as fast as possible. Trust the good people of Southwark, Toby. They are sick and tired of Hemlock and his evil ways. And Sally's name carries a huge amount of respect.'

He then faced Inky and Herbert. 'Right chaps, we've a lot to do. And you Toby, you get over to the Globe and organize the men as they arrive.'

'But-'

'No buts, lad. We know the area far better than you do. And we need someone who knows the situation when the men start to arrive.'

A thick fog draped across the city as Burbage, Inky and Herbert took to the streets. Toby – feeling a thousand misgivings, and with his nerves stretched to breaking point – seriously doubted anybody would turn up at the Globe? Sixty minutes later his doubts were transformed to beliefs when dozens of stagehands, actors, and tradesmen, plus an assortment of Hemlock's past victims and sworn enemies, crammed around the Globe stage.

'Pray tell, Toby,' beamed a mightily pleased looking Burbage. 'Will this number suffice, do you think?'

'Oh, I think it will more than suffice,' said an astonished Toby.

'Righto then,' said Burbage. 'Let's get this 'meeting' organized!' And straightaway a rousing chorus of hoots and cheers filled the theatre.

'Hemlock will be here in about ten minutes,' said Toby. 'It's likely he will have his most trusted men with him: Inky reckons twelve or thirteen at most. Do you guys think we can handle that?'

The men looked at each other as if they'd just heard a joke – and burst out laughing.

'Don't you worry, lad,' smiled Stinky McGinnty, as he doled-out a cache of rocks from a sack. 'These little pain-inducers will do all the handling that's required.'

'Aye, and iffin they don't, this hammer surely will…' a roaring Mincer Crabtree waved a great sledge-hammer in the air – much to the cheering delight of his allies.

'And you may have noticed, Toby,' said Growler Mullion, shouldering a sledge-hammer of his own. 'These are not pink or made of glass.'

Another blast of shouty cheers echoed around the Globe.

'Shush everybody!' Burbage said hurriedly. 'Hide as best you can in the balconies. And as soon we give the signal, dive in and let them have it. But remember, we're here to rescue Miss Sally, not injure her. So be as careful as you can.'

As Toby and the boys ducked behind the huge stage pillars – Stinky, Growler and Mincer, along with the rest of the men, scattered themselves along the balconies.

Five seconds later the sounds of men approaching the Globe could clearly be heard. Hemlock's voice barked an order.

'Spoon – check it out.'

Ned Spoon crept forward and nudged open the big entrance doors of the Globe. Satisfied with a swift look around, he departed.

'There's nobody, Boss. Its empty.'

'Right you lot, pin your ears back. You know the drill. As soon as they arrive we hit them with everything we've got. But leave the writer to me: he's all mine.'

Moments later a cluster of shadowy figures shuffled their way through the huge doors. Last in line was Hemlock with a frail looking Sally trailing behind on the end of a rope. There were dark rings under her eyes and her face looked deathly pale and frightened. Seeing her in such distress only served to pump-up Toby and the would-be rescuers. It was time for action. The show to beat all shows was about to open at the Globe.

'Now, everybody…' Toby roared, jumping out onto the stage.

'CHAAAAAAAAAAAAARRRGGEEE…'

Pandemonium ensued as years of pent-up anger rained down mercilessly upon the hoodlums. First came an avalanche of rocks, stones, sticks and hammers, quickly followed by an onslaught of thumps, wallops and kicks. Panic-stricken and disorientated, it was like the madman Olympics as hoodlums trampled over each other in desperate efforts to escape. At least two gangsters managed to fire-off a couple of shots in the general direction of Burbage and Toby. One of the rounds exploded into a pillar an inch from Toby's head, sending splinters of wood flying through the air. Mincer and Stinky quickly put paid to the shooters.

With such a united force of men supporting each other, the battle was over almost as quickly as it began. One by one the gangsters were battered, bruised and utterly defeated – except for Ned Spoon. He realized almost at once where the trouble had started, and charged at Toby like a furious bull.

'AGHHHHHHHHH' he roared, while moving with astonishing speed and brandishing a knife as big as a sword.

At the very last second, and much to Toby's relief, Spoon disappeared down the stage trapdoor.

'Gotcha!' laughed Burbage from backstage, his hand holding the trapdoor lever.

A great heap of stunned gangsters lay piled high in front of the stage as cheers of victory echoed through the theatre. The cheering, however, didn't last long.

'Look there!' shouted Toby, pointing madly at the exit doors. 'That swine Hemlock is escaping with Sally!'

It was too late to stop Hemlock – he had already disappeared into the misty night. Toby felt devastated: all their efforts had been a waste.

'Don't worry, lad,' said Mincer. 'The only place he can head for is his hideout down by the river. And I know exactly where it is. Let's go!'

Along with Toby, Inky and Herbert, and a posse of yelling workers behind him, Mincer charged through the doors in the direction of the river. A sudden a scream cut through the night and everyone stopped dead in their tracks.

'That's Sally!' Toby cried. 'Everyone shush!'

Cupping their ears Toby and Inky crouched down and listened intently. Hemlock's harsh roaring voice could just about be heard.

'He's not so far away!' Inky exclaimed, taking off

like a rocket in the direction of the scream. 'Follow me, Toby.'

'We'll head in the other direction with Mincer's crew and try to cut him off!' Herbert called after Toby, before haring away to the left.

And that's where things went disastrously wrong for Toby. In his frantic efforts to keep up with Inky, he tripped and stumbled straight out into the pitch-black abyss over the icy Thames.

'Nooooooooooooo!' he shrieked, his hands clawing furiously for something, anything, to grab.

At the very last moment his fingers found a rope dangling from a dockside crane. He gripped it with all his strength. But still, such was the force of his momentum he was propelled in a great swerving arc across the river.

24. COME-UPPANCE

Like phantom silhouettes, Hemlock and Sally shuffled along the empty quaysides. Woozy and distressed, Sally had no idea where they were or where they were going. She shivered all over. Just then, as a lonely shaft of moonlight sparkled on the frosty ground, she heard voices calling.

It was her name.

Voices were calling her name.

For a few wonderful seconds her heart filled with hope.

Not for the first time, however, did she stumble and fall, only for Hemlock to drag her, screaming, along the ground.

'So help me, wench,' he snarled. 'One more squawk out of you and it will be your last!'

There was a new cruelty in his voice, a sound so nasty it made the hairs on the back of Sally's neck rise up. Hemlock didn't have to threaten her a second time.

Minutes later they had arrived at their destination. Sally could hardly believe it. They were back at the lair. And before she could begin to take it all in, Hemlock was crashing through the front door.

'I have no idea how they arranged that little performance,' he roared, throwing Sally aside. 'But mark my words retribution will be swift and severe.'

Calculating that news of his downfall would be spreading rapidly, and that his many enemies could arrive at any minute seeking revenge, he needed to work fast. Grabbing a shovel, he began digging at the floor like a starving dog looking for a bone.

'This is just a tactical withdrawal,' he jabbered, his voice shrill with anger. 'And heaven help those who crossed me this night. I will skin them alive when I return – I swear it. And *you*, Shakespeare, you won't have long to wait to know my vengeance. Your nice little family will pay for your effrontery.'

Minutes later he threw the shovel aside and began stuffing gold and silver coins into bags and money-belts. When finished he strapped the weighty loot across his shoulders and around his waist.

'It's time to get going again,' he ordered, hauling Sally to her feet and pushing her through the door.

'But surely you don't need me now, Mr Hemlock?' she reasoned. 'You should let me go, I'll only slow you down.'

'You are my insurance in case your associates attempt to interrupt my departure plans.'

'Mr. Hemlock, nobody will bother you once you leave me here, I promise you that.'

Hemlock laughed. 'Allow me to give you some free advice. Never put your faith in promises: especially those made by a prisoner.'

'But Mr. Hemlock, I assure you…'

Hemlock slapped Sally across the face.

'Begging is pointless. So from here on, you will do exactly as I say and nothing else. Do you understand?'

'Y-Yes, sir. I understand.'

'Good… Now. Let's get moving.'

Huge black clouds rolled across the city as they made their way along the deserted waterfronts. On and on they struggled, until eventually they came to a halt alongside a lonely wharf.

'Here at last,' Hemlock said, peering gleefully across

the squally blackness of the Thames estuary.

Pulling Sally forward they clambered down a slimy ladder onto a timber jetty that jutted out over the fast-flowing river. A small skiff bumped gently against the mooring.

'What's that?' Sally asked fretfully. 'You don't expect me to get into that thing?'

As Icy beads of rain stung her face like tiny electric shocks, Sally watched Hemlock's shape move menacingly across the jetty.

'You're going to kill me, aren't you?' she said quietly, her lungs swelling and emptying in mounting terror.

'No choice, I'm afraid.' Hemlock answered tiredly. 'I can't bring you with me. More importantly, your demise will act as a warning to those who have crossed me this fine day.'

'Please let me go, Mr. Hemlock!'

'Regrettably I cannot do that. I wish I could, but…'

The extra weight of his loot made the timbers groan as he stepped towards Sally. All at once he halted. An eerie sound was billowing in from the river? Momentarily intrigued, Hemlock squinted out through the darkness. The sound was getting louder and louder and closer and closer. To his amazement, slicing through the night air, a ghostly apparition was zooming towards him on the end of a rope.

'…nooooOOOOOOOW' the apparition wailed before crashing headlong into Hemlock.

Utterly winded Hemlock stumbled backwards, his sinewy arms flaying about madly as he tried to stop himself from falling. It was no use. In the blink of an eye he had staggered backwards off the jetty and hit the river with a dull splush.

It was the last sound the gangster ever made.

For a few despairing seconds, while being swept away by the fast-flowing tide, Hemlock flapped, flopped and splashed. Finally, inexorably, owing to the weight of the silver and gold, he slipped beneath the choppy water like a stone.

'W-What just happened…?' Sally stammered, staring incredulously at the flying apparition, now slumped in front of her.

'Good grief. Is that you, Toby?'

'Eh…. yes…I think it is,' Toby wheezed, pushing himself onto his elbows.

'Oh Toby – Toby!' Sally beamed, hugging him like crazy. 'You saved my life.'

The others arrived just in time to witness the scene.

'How'd you do that?' Inky asked, scratching his head. 'How did you get here before us? I mean, one minute you're behind us, and the next…?'

'Who cares how he did it,' Sally shouted joyfully. 'He saved me *and* got rid of Hemlock at the same time.'

Although he willingly accepted Sally's gushing accolades, Toby had no idea what she was talking about?

'Pffff – think nothing of it,' he shrugged, while Sally helped him to his feet. 'The big question is, Sally. How are you?'

'Oh I'm fine!' Sally answered breezily. 'It would take more than a one-eyed homicidal maniac to scare me.'

'Attagirl,' Toby proudly declared – and they had a big nervous laugh together.

Inky edged close to the water's edge. 'He's really gone for good, isn't he?'

'Got that right.' Sally said. 'Unless he managed to turn into a fish, he's well and truly gone.'

*

The news that Hemlock was indeed gone for good, spread faster than a greyhound with six legs. And if Sally was hugely admired before, she was now a superhero – and Toby wasn't far behind.

Celebrations were the order of the evening as the entire Southwark neighbourhood spontaneously started a party. By midnight the fun and frolics, much like the fog rolling in from the river, had spread across the Globe. Not everybody, however, was having a great time.

'You ok, Sal,' Toby asked, noticing Sally looked down in the dumps.

'Yes, I suppose,' she replied, a hint of sadness in her voice.

'You only suppose?'

'To be honest, Toby. I'm still very shaken with all that craziness today.'

'Perfectly understandable.'

Sally's voice dropped almost to a whisper. 'I know it's perfectly understandable. But to be even more honest, there's something on my mind that won't stop bothering me.'

'Yeah... go on?'

'It's what Hemlock said before you kicked his sorry backside into the Thames. I can't get it out of my mind.'

'What did he say?'

'He was rambling on about how Mr. Shakespeare's family would pay a price for his so-called *effrontery*. The thing is – I don't believe he was just rambling. He really meant it... like it was a done deal.'

'Sal. He can't hurt anyone anymore. He's gone. For good. So really, there's no need to worry.'

'Toby. I saw him go down with my own eyes. But I

still can't shake off this horrible feeling. If only there was some way we could find out what's happening in Stratford. Its times like this I wish phones were invented.'

Wrinkling his face, Toby shrugged. 'Sal. I have a gut feeling everything is ok, even in Stratford.'

'Really, Toby?'

'I wouldn't say it if I didn't mean it.'

'Ok, maybe I am worrying unnecessarily. Maybe everything *is* all right and I should try to put all that nonsense out of my mind.'

Right at that moment, as gales of laughter erupted from the Globe like fountains of fun, Sally did begin to feel better. Alas her good feelings didn't last for long. A sudden undispellable sense of dread rushed through her as the crunching sound of hobnailed boots approached. Looking around anxiously, she had to stifle a scream when the towering figures of Bloodnutt materialised out of the swirling fog.

'Well blow me down!' he said, beaming like a bear who'd stumbled across a free meal.

'Talk about convenient. I thought I'd be kicking down doors and smashing a few heads before I found you two.'

The iron fists of Bilge and Splatt pushed Toby and Sally to their knees. Stooping down, Bloodnutt stared into Toby's ashen face.

'You remember me, don'tcha lad?' he said, comically rotating his head at different angles. 'Surely you haven't forgotten my handsome mush. Come along, now. What's my name?'

Toby could barely get the words out. 'You're Mr. Bloodnutt, sir.'

'Bravo!' Bloodnutt cheered. 'From here on, though, you only speak when I tells you to. Is that understood?'

'Yes sir, understand... *stood*, I mean, sir,' answered

Toby. 'But I really don't know what you---'

A punch to his stomach poleaxed Toby.

'Like I said, you speak when I tells you to. Now, pay attention. The dogs on the street know you put an end to my old mucker, Hemlock. Don't get me wrong. I'm impressed, and I understand why you did it. I mean, he was your deadliest enemy: and who wouldn't want to get rid of their deadliest enemy. Tis only natural. Unfortunately you crossed a line when you made-off with his gold and silver. Because you see, most of that was mine. And now I wants it back. In fact I wants it *all* back.'

Toby, afraid to open his mouth, looked questioningly at Bloodnutt.

'Ok, you can speak now.'

'I swear to you on the biggest stack of bibles, Mr. Bloodnutt. I have no idea where Mr. Hemlock's gold is?'

'Which is exactly what I expected to hear. And if I were in your boots, I'd be saying the same thing.'

'But I'm telling you the truth, Mr. Bloodnutt. I can't give what I haven't got?'

'If that's the way you want to play it, fine by me. Although I'm sure a couple of days as my personal guest in the Tower will loosen your tongue.'

A nod at his henchmen, and Bilge and Splatt had Toby gagged, blindfolded and tethered. Bloodnutt turned his attention to Sally, her terrified face streaked with tears.

'As for you, my pretty girl. Your luck is in. I need someone to act as a go-between, and you're it.'

'Mr. Bloodnutt, please. You must believe Toby. He really doesn't know anything about Mr. Hemlock's gold. As far as I can tell he took it with him when he drowned.'

Bloodnutt responded with a lazy smile and a shrug of his huge shoulders.

'Lying through your teeth won't help your friend, m'dear. And believe me, every minute he spends at the Tower will be hell on earth for him. So unless you change your mind and give me the information I want – Master Sprocket will never see daylight again. I'll leave you to mull things over. I expect to hear from you soon… or not. You decide.'

To the sound of Sally's sobbing, Bloodnutt and his sidekicks disappeared through the fog with Toby in tow as quickly as they had appeared.

When Inky and Herbert arrived, and Sally told them what had happened, they could hardly believe their ears.

'Let's catch them up!' Inky demanded, his small muscular frame primed and ready to chase after Bloodnutt.

Herbert's eyes narrowed in careful thought.

'Eh, wouldn't be a good move, Inky. It would probably cause more harm than good. We need to think this out carefully. If we make the wrong decision, Toby will pay the price.'

'Yes, you're right.' Inky agreed. 'Still… I think this whole set-up stinks. There is nothing legal or official about any of it. I reckon it's Bloodnutt's personal little enterprise. And if that's the case we really do need to come up with a plan, and a good one at that.'

'But that makes zero sense,' said Sally, shaking her head. 'If it's illegal, why can't we just go and report him to whoever runs the Tower?'

'Because, Sally. By the time they check the situation, Toby would be a dead man. Bloodnutt would see to that.'

'Herbert is right. Also, how would we prove it? It would be our word against the word of a Tower guard. We mustn't blunder our way into this. As long as Bloodnutt believes Toby has the gold, he will be safe.'

25. THE ASSASSIN

Tom Shiner, renowned blacksmith and firearms expert, swung his lean body away from the supper table.

'You must be in a mile-o-trouble, Will Shakespeare – to be out and about looking for a pistol and a horse?'

Squeezing himself from the table, Mr. Shakespeare stood by the fireplace, pausing to gaze at the ornaments along the mantlepiece.

'To be honest, Tom,' he said, an edge of sadness in his voice.

'I'm not a hundred per cent sure *what* I want. The next 24 hours will tell all. And as for the pistol… it's more a precaution than anything else.'

'Phuu… tis a mighty powerful precaution. Anyhow, let's go see what we can do for you.'

The blacksmith steered his friend through a back yard and a small lean-to workshop. In wavering lamplight he rummaged through neatly arranged stacks and shelves of tools and equipment. In due course he rooted out a leather pouch, carefully unwrapped it, and revealed an immaculate pair of flintlock pistols.

'Ordinarily, to make proper use of these weapons would require serious practice,' Tom Shiner explained, pensively stroking his beard. 'But since you're in such a secret hurry, a brief tutorial will have to suffice.'

In the faint light of a waning moon the blacksmith carefully loaded and primed the weapons.

'All you need to do now, Will – is cock the hammers… aim… and pull the triggers. Which for your sake, I hope you won't have to do.'

Shakespeare shoved the pistols into his trouser belt. 'Trust me, Tom. I feel exactly the same.'

'Right so, let's see about that horse,' continued Shiner, walking out along the yard.

The stable block, with its fodder shelves, saddle hooks and a great store of straw, was big enough to house a dozen horses. At the gable end were three tethered mounts lazily chewing their evening feed of oats. Using a gentle voice the blacksmith untied a big chestnut mare with strong legs and a blazing white star on her forehead.

'Normally I wouldn't lend old Nessy to a knighted prince,' he began while fastening a saddle to her back. 'But I know you'll take great care with her.'

Wrapping his capes and scarves around himself like an onion, Shakespeare clambered into the saddle.

'Worry not, my friend,' he said, leaning over to pull and tighten the stirrups. 'I will do all in my power to bring her home safe and sound. For now though, all I can say is thank you for what you've done.'

With the scrape of iron on cobblestone and the clink of bridle and bit, Nessy clip-clopped her way through the foggy streets of London. Before long they reached the mud and grass of open countryside, and trusting her not to run off a cliff or down a bog hole, Mr. Shakespeare drove Nessy to full gallop.

With impressive speed they charged into the night – jumping streams, ditches and hedgerows, and hurtling past wide-eyed travellers who swore at them for nearly running them over. Onward they raced through woodlands of oak, chestnut and silver birch, their trunks gleaming in the moonlight, until many hours later, as dawn cracked across a new horizon, they finally reached the outskirts of Stratford-upon-Avon.

Slipping down from Nessy's back, plastered now in

steaming sweat, Mr. Shakespeare led her to a field with lush green grass and a cool stream running through it.

'Thank you, girl,' he smiled, as dawn shone on his tired face. 'You are a queen among horses.'

Gathering what strength he had left he jogged over the stone bridge that crossed the river Avon. Thatched roofs nudged their way through a morning mist when Shakespeare eventually reached the garden path to his house on Chapel Street. The sheer relief of catching sight of his smiling wife and their new granddaughter washed over him like a mountain stream. All was seemingly well in that quiet corner of Warwickshire.

Slumping down on the grey stone lintel by the front door, his aching body reminded him that he was no longer a young man. Calm suddenly changed to concern, however, when the small silence of the morning was cut short by the snap of a twig. Jumping to his feet Shakespeare listened and listened. Had he imagined it? Was he merely overtired? No… there it was again, only closer this time. Straining his eyes he glimpsed a shadow advancing rapidly towards the house. In the misty half-light his instincts immediately took over.

'Halt where you are, stranger,' he ordered commandingly. 'I am armed and will not hesitate to stop you.'

The shadowy figure paused beneath an oak tree, but only in surprise and just for a moment. Satisfied he was in no danger, he lunged forward unwaveringly.

For reasons Shakespeare could not later explain, he reacted with calm unerring composure. In a smooth unhurried arc he cocked the pistols, took aim, and fired both together. One shot zinged harmlessly past the figure's right ear while the other blasted into his left kneecap. The figure instantly fell to the ground shrieking like a goblin.

'Me knee! Me knee!' he cried. 'You shot me bloody knee off!'

The Shakespeare family, running out to investigate such a frightful disturbance, were shocked to find Mr. Shakespeare standing there shaking like a leaf with a pair of smoking pistols in his hands. Even more shocking was a hooded individual screaming at his feet.

'Oh my lord, Will. What have you got yourself into?' cried a distraught Mrs. Shakespeare.

Her husband could barely speak. 'H-He was attacking the house. I had no choice, you understand. No choice… *no* choice…'

While every dog within a radius of three miles was barking like crazy, most of Stratford's population were running towards Chapel Street. Finding a hooded stranger wailing in agony was the last thing they expected. Not only was the stranger dressed entirely in black he was also armed to the teeth with weapons of every description.

'Obviously an evil-doer of the worst kind,' was the general consensus after the stranger was bandaged-up and taken into custody.

'It was only Gods-given luck,' Mrs Shakespeare explained to her neighbours. 'That my William had chosen this very night for a surprise visit. I can't imagine what might have happened if he hadn't.'

While she chatted on, her husband's heart was filled with fear and concern. Tears fell from his eyes. He knew what he must do: what was best for all concerned.

'Will, are you feeling all right?' his wife asked.

'No, Anne. I-I am not,' he stammered, the reality of recent events flooding his mind. 'I must get back to London, today…this minute even…'

Before he could move an inch towards London, however, he fainted from shock and exhaustion.

It was twelve hours before he resurfaced and found the incident of the previous night was still being gossiped, blabbered, and jabbered about.

'I need a walk to clear my mind,' an edgy Shakespeare explained to his wife before strolling out of range from chin-wagging neighbours.

Soon enough he reached the Old Reindeer Inn and the warm welcoming glow of an open fire. To help his mind-clearing process, a mug of ale in a quiet inconspicuous corner was made use of. A few minutes of solitude later his attention was drawn towards the bar. Manly gossip and sweet-smelling pipe smoke filled the air as three local men engaged in a discussion about events near and far.

'...kilt in a sword fight I heard,' an older man commented. 'And his body thrun in the Thames.'

'Horsefeathers!' a younger man contradicted. 'It were a duel with blunderbusses. Blowed his head clean off his shoulders, he did.'

For one annoying moment Shakespeare thought last night's events were being overly embellished. He shoved himself further into the corner.

'Well, one thing's for sure,' the older man continued with a slow nod. 'Satan will never be lonely with the likes of Christian Hemlock at his side. Now he's dead and gone, London will be a safer place.'

'Aye, and what were that lads name again,' remarked the younger man. 'The one that kilt him?'

'Ohhh... what were it, now. Locket? Or...or...or maybe Pocket?'

Shakespeare jumped to his feet.

'SPROCKET!' he shouted, stabbing a finger into the

air as if answering an especially difficult pub-quiz question.

Such an unexpectedly loud intrusion made the older man splutter and spill his drink.

'I do beg your pardon,' said Shakespeare. 'But I couldn't help overhearing your news about Hemlock. Are you absolutely sure it was Hemlock... Christian Hemlock... *and* that he is dead?'

'Oh I be sure all right,' the man replied, leaning on the bar. 'I heard it from a man who heard from his cousin who got it from the horse's mouth: and *he* saw it happen. The news be all over London.'

'And the lad you mentioned earlier. Could it have been Sprocket. Toby Sprocket?'

'Toe-bee-Sprocket?' the older man repeated slowly. 'Aye, sure enough, that were it... Toe-bee Sprocket... he kilt Hemlock stone dead, he did.'

26. A GREAT ESCAPE

Confused and groggy, Toby dragged himself awake. He blinked. He blinked again. He waved a hand an inch from his face... and there was nothing there? Nothing but blackness. A shadow painted black could not be as blacker. Something cold touched his ankle – it was a slithery snake of terror crawling up his leg.

'Aiieeeee...I'm blinded...I'm blinded...!' he screamed, falling back against a cold wall oozing with slime.

Before he went completely doolally he noticed a wonderful sight down by his feet. It was a faint glow, perhaps a tiny chink of daylight. Falling to his knees he found a gap at the bottom of the thick wooden door. Thank heavens – it *was* a chink of daylight.

With his panic-levels returning to normal, Toby tried patching together what had happened after being snatched. There were blurred memories of being carried under a stone arch, being kicked and punched and being hauled down a flight of granite steps. Finally there was this awful darkness.

'Holy mother, I remember now,' he told himself. 'I'm in a cell in the Tower of London. I'm a friggin prisoner!'

The cell was empty: no bed, no water, no food, nothing but slimy walls and putrid smells. Hours dripped along... and along....and along. The air felt solid and heavy, relentlessly pressing down on him. A scream echoed up from the bowels of the Tower. Toby screamed back even louder. Then something peculiar happened. The floor, gloomy and vague, seemed to be moving. To his horror he discovered the floor was teeming with bugs and creepie-crawlies – and the more he kicked and hooshed them away the more they scurried back in droves.

To block all that from his mind, he tried to dream-up a cunning escape plan. But no matter how hard he imagined and mulled and pondered, a doable plan refused to materialise.

'Pretend!' he yelled suddenly. 'That's what I'll do… I'll pretend I've gone nuts and take whatever chances that might create.'

As escape plans go it wasn't the cleverest – but considering the predicament he was in, it wasn't the worst either.

'What I wouldn't do for a bowl of *Mutton à la Blyster!*' he sighed hungrily when his empty belly gurgled. In fact, he was so hungry he seriously considered snacking on a few creepy-crawlies, maybe even that especially big cockroach he found crawling through his hair.

'Hey little pal,' he smiled, his eyes almost accustomed to the gloom. 'You lost as well?'

A jingling of keys startled him. It was Bilge and Splatt coming to collect their prize. Toby winked at the wriggling cockroach and shoved him into his shirt pocket.

'You've had enough lazing about in this fine apartment, my lad,' Splatt shouted. 'It's time to earn your keep.'

They dragged Toby so fast up the stairs his knees smashed into every granite step along the way. In due course he was flung into a yard where sunlight burned into his eyes like a laser.

'Well, Mr. Bilge,' said Splatt. 'Methinks Master

Sprocket is in for a very uncomfortable afternoon.'

'Aye, that's true,' Bilge replied tersely. 'I'd hate to be in his boots and no mistake.'

With his foul-smelling breath wafting over Toby's face, Splatt leaned in close. 'But guess what, Sprocket. If you play your cards right we could help you escape. Would you like to know how?'

'Oh yes please!' Toby answered childishly.

'Listen closely then. If you tell *us* where the gold is, we'll show you the secret way out of here. What do you say to that?'

It was time for Toby to put his insanity plan into action. He reached into his shirt pocket and pulled out the cockroach.

'This is Bugsy!' he smiled stupidly, holding the cockroach up for inspection. 'Say thank-you to the nice man for helping us escape, Bugsy.'

The guards looked blankly at each other, and then burst into hooting laughter. While still laughing they dragged Toby to a small room at the back of the guardhouse.

'Here he is, Sarge,' Bilge declared, flinging Toby roughly to the floor.

Bloodnutt went ballistic when he saw the state Toby was in. 'I warned you not to push him too far.' he snarled, grabbing Bilge by the throat. 'I warned you… I *warned* you!'

'But sir…' Bilge wheezed, his face turning blue.

'Shaaaaduuuup!!' Bloodnutt roared, flinging Bilge aside. 'I'm giving both of you fair warning. If this little rat dies before he talks, I'll kick you both over the north tower. Now… bilge, go get some water.'

The very idea of water filled Toby with joy. Wisely he controlled his reactions to eavesdrop into a very interesting conversation.

'....alls I'm saying is,' Splatt said, with an edgy look over his shoulder. 'We can't keep him here forever. Pepper has been watching us like a hawk.'

'Don't you worry your tiny brains about old fancy-pants,' he fumed, his eyes swelling-out like balloons. 'I'll deal with him when the time comes. All you need to worry about is Sprocket.'

Bilge arrived back with water. And as he poured it over the prisoner's wobbly head, Toby gulped down as much as possible while pretending not to want it.

'Put him in the chair,' Bloodnutt barked. 'It's time to deal with this properly.'

'Open your eyes afore I cut your lids off,' he barked, flashing a knife in front of Toby.

'Oh hello there...' Toby smiled dazedly, as he extracted the cockroach from his shirt pocket. 'Have you met my friend, Bugsy?'

Bloodnutt whacked the cockroach from his hand and slapped Toby so hard he heard bells ringing.

'I don't have time for stupid games, Sprocket. So I'll make this simple for you. Tell me where the gold is, and you live – if you don't, you die.'

Toby maintained a stupid grin on his face. 'Has Bugsy gone then, mister?'

Bloodnutt slapped Toby again. This time so hard, Toby flew head over heels off the chair.

'Where is the gold?' Bloodnutt screamed.

'Bugsy! Help! Help!'

Another slap followed, then another, and another...

Toby quickly realised that pretending to be insane was not having the desired effect. In an instant he changed tack. It would be his last throw of the dice.

Jutting his chin out, he sat bolt upright and glared

defiantly into Bloodnutt's sweating face.

'Bloodnutt,' he said slowly and calmly. 'Are you really that stupid, or are you just practicing?'

'Huh…?'

'I suppose if you have a face like a pig's arse you might also have the brains of a pig's arse.'

'W-What's that you say?' Bloodnutt spluttered, completely taken aback.

'I said, you have a face like a pig's arse. And I don't mean that as an insult, I'm simply stating a fact. But it's not your fault: it's biology, you were just born that way.'

'Why you little---'

'…hold it!' Toby ordered, pinching Bloodnutt's lips together between thumb and forefinger.

'You're dead right about one thing. I do know where the gold is. But you will never make me tell you: not without your pet monkeys to back you up,' Toby guffawed, pointing his thumb at Bilge and Splatt.

'Even Hemlock couldn't do that. He didn't stand a chance against me. And you know what? Man-to-man you wouldn't stand a chance either.'

A collective intake of breath emptied the guardroom of oxygen. Bilge and Splatt were astounded. Never before had their sergeant been challenged like that. And it definitely was a challenge.

For one horrifying moment Toby thought smoke was spewing out of Bloodnutt's ears. It was all Toby could do to stop his mouth from screaming.

'Bilge, Splatt. Get out of the room.'

'But sir, he hasn't said where---'

'----get out of here, *NOW!*' Bloodnutt growled through gritted teeth. Bilge and Splatt fell over themselves in a mad rush to vacate the guardroom.

Without taking his eyes off Toby, Bloodnutt removed

his leather jerkin and rolled-up his sleeves.

'I don't get it,' he said quizzically, 'Why would an insect like you challenge someone like me to a fight. I mean…. *you* against *me?*'

'Listen, bum-face. Are we gonna talk all day or get down to business.'

Bloodnutt laughed evilly. 'Okay fine – but you've just signed your own death warrant. I'm gonna pulverize your brains and pull your guts out through your ears.'

'Yeah, well…. I-I'm gonna do something really nasty to you as well… so like, you better watch out, yeah.'

Like wild beasts they began circling each other. Well, maybe one wild beast and a shivering mass of human jelly. Bloodnutt, his arm muscles squirming like a bag of eels, made a grab for Toby's neck. Toby dodged to the right, then to the left, and then, unbelievably, he dived straight out the open window.

Crash-landing on Bilge and Splatt, Toby knocked them over into a confused heap. Without missing a beat, he took off like a bullet, scattering a flock of ravens and startling a squad of passing guards as he went.

'Stop him – stop him, you fools!' Bloodnutt roared, kicking Bilge and Splatt into action.

But it was too late.

The prisoner had well and truly scarpered.

Toby hadn't a clue where he was going – he just wanted to put as much distance as possible between himself and that lunatic Bloodnutt. All he could think of was maybe jumping into the Thames and swimming to freedom. Roughly calculating where the river might be, he charged off in that direction.

'Arrest that man!' Captain Pepper yelled when he caught sight of a stranger running past his office window.

By that stage Toby was so desperate he began clawing

and jumping at the north wall like a rat caught in a barrel. A dozen guards rushed after the crazy little stranger trying to run up the wall. Vice-like fingers easily pinned him to the ground, thus ending Toby's escape attempt.

'Who are you and where in the King's name did you come from?' the astonished captain asked.

'My name... is Sprocket... and I came... from one of your cells... sir.'

The captain looked hard at Toby. He turned to the guards. 'Do any of you know this prisoner?'

When the response he got was a gaggle of confused looks, the captain knew something was seriously amiss. Bloodnutt, slow-brained as he was, understood the game was up. All he could do now was grab his loot and get out of town as fast as possible.

Scurrying back to his quarters he frantically began stuffing his getaway bags. Bilge and Splatt soon joined him.

'Where the devil where you two?' he barked, rushing about the guardroom. 'Saddle my horse and bring him round here now!'

Instead of obeying orders, the two guards, pale and frightened, continued standing there quaking in their boots. Splatt cleared his throat.

'Eh, sarge. What about us then. Aren't we leaving with you?'

Bloodnutt faced the hapless duo.

'What! You two! leaving with me! Have you lost your minds. It's every man for himself now. So get that horse saddled-up before I take my sword to you.'

While Bloodnutt continued his frenzied packing, Bilge and Splatt looked dazedly at each other. With their hopes utterly dashed, Bilge sneakily grabbed a bedpan poking out from under Bloodnutt's bed, and with great force brought it whizzing down on the sergeant's thick skull. A resounding GOOOOOONG echoed all the way down to the river. Bloodnutt's reign of terror had been brought an abrupt and ignominious end.

Hijacking their leader's ill-gotten gains, Bilge and Splatt were skedaddling off towards the Tower gates, when Captain Pepper and a squad of armed guards suddenly appeared.

'Hold it right there, you two!'

'I-It weren't our fault, captain, sir,' Bilge hysterically blurted. 'The sergeant made us do it, he made us work for Hemlock and Spoon and all dem others.'

A confused captain stared at the trembling duo.

'What on earth are you talking about. I simply want you to help search the grounds?'

'Oh-Oh!' said Bilge, looking bewildered.

The captain pulled out his sword.

'I think we should have a little chat, boys. And perhaps we should start with this Hemlock story.'

27. SURPRISE SURPRISE

'We have to face facts.' Herbert said glumly. 'It's almost noon and the longer we sit around here the harder it's going to get for Toby.'

'I wholeheartedly agree,' said Burbage, pacing up and down the room. 'Therefore the only logical course of action left to us now, is a direct approach to the Tower to plead our case. We must, however, try to make sure we see the *right* people. I will leave immediately and make the necessary arrangements.'

'But all that could take hours?' Sally said pleadingly. 'Hours that Toby will be suffering even more at the hands of that brute.'

'Be that as it may, my dear,' said Burbage, pulling on his hat and cape. 'At this late stage I don't see any other way of dealing with it.'

A violent hammering on the door brought proceedings to a nerve-jangling stop.

'Oh please no,' Sally moaned, closing her eyes. 'Not more bad news, I can't take more bad news.'

Inky made his way up the hall and dragged the door open. A muffled rumpus of brawny voices ensued, quickly followed by a clumping of feet marching towards the kitchen. Sally put a trembling hand to her mouth when a fierce looking military man entered the kitchen.

'Am I addressing Ms. Sally Bunn?' he loudly inquired.

'Yes…sir?'

'Well then, I believe you might know this chap!' captain Pepper announced smilingly. And in stepped

Toby, grinning like an idiot.

For a split-second Sally thought she was seeing things.

'Toby!' she squealed, almost knocking Herbert over in her rush towards Toby. 'You're free! You're free!'

Herbert and Inky were equally amazed.

'I don't understand...' Inky said. 'How? I mean *how?*'

'Perhaps I may answer that,' the captain proposed. 'Master Sprocket was unlawfully detained at the Tower of London by a renegade sergeant of the guard. Fortunately he managed to outwit his captor *and* a pair of back-stabbing weasel guards. For his assistance in bringing these traitors to justice the Tower will forever be grateful. I can see you are anxious to celebrate his homecoming, so I shall leave you to it.' And with that, the captain saluted smartly and marched out of their lives forever.

A great cheer erupted as Toby was swamped with hugs, back-slaps, and handshakes.

'This is fantastic!' said Herbert. 'We were going out of our tiny minds with worry.'

'And talk about stealing the limelight,' laughed Inky. 'Sally saves the Globe, and you get rid of Hemlock and Bloodnutt. What's next on the menu I wonder?'

'I'll tell you what's next on the menu,' said Toby. 'A big fat fried-egg sandwich followed by *another* big fat fried-egg sandwich.'

'Oh no, it's not,' said Sally, waggling her finger. 'You stink to high heaven. So first, you need a good wash.'

'But I'm *star*ving!'

'I'm sure you are, Toby. Unfortunately my sense of smell can't take the pressure. So... You do the washing and I'll make the sandwich. Also just to let you know, the *Winter's Tale* is opening at the Globe today. And if you're up for a day out, Mrs. Blyster has cleaned and pressed our old clothes.'

*

Toby scrubbed himself clean and donned his freshly cleaned old clothes. They felt really good against his skin and starkly reminded him of home.

'Hey there,' Sally said smilingly, entering the attic. 'I figured you couldn't wait. So here's a double fried egg sarni and a mug of cold milk.'

'Let me at it!' Toby drooled, raking back his wet hair and grabbing the food.

'I was just thinking,' he said between huge mouthfuls. 'I know I'm tired and all. But I really would love to catch the opening at the Globe.'

'Great!' Sally said, jumping up to go downstairs. 'We'll head out as soon as you're…. you're….'

Sally had come to an abrupt halt. Standing motionless for a moment, she reversed slowly backwards, and stared into the cockpit of the Mark 5 .

'You ok, Sal?'

'Those lights,' she said quickly. 'Should they be like that – flashing, I mean?'

'What flashing lights?'

'*Those* flashing lights,' she repeated, pointing shakily.

Toby rushed over and looked into the machine. His eyes almost popped out of his head.

'I-I don't believe it,' he stuttered. 'The power… it's back on. IT'S BACK ON!'

The cockpit lights were indeed flashing and sparkling

like a crate of beautiful electronic jewels: exactly like on that momentous day back in the lab. Hurling himself at the canopy, Toby pulled it open. A soothing pulsating hum spilled out into the attic. It felt heady and warm and wonderful.

'This is totally amazing,' Toby laughed, dragging his hands slowly down his face. 'The grid. It's almost fully charged. I reckon another couple of hours and it'll be powered-up completely.'

'But how did that happen?' Sally asked. 'I don't get it.'

'Me neither!' Toby shrugged, holding his head then with his hands. 'No,no,no, hold on a minute. I-I think I'm starting to remember!'

'Remember what?' Sally queried, feeling slightly scared by Toby's reaction.

In the dusty shelves of Toby's brain, memories and recollections were tumbling together. Thinking back to that last day, it felt like his mind was recovering from a fever of forgetfulness.

He slapped his forehead.

'"Keep it fully closed" Unc said. "Keep the canopy *fully* closed and the batteries will automatically recharge themselves." I remember! I remember! And that's exactly what you did a couple of nights ago, Sally. You *fully* closed the canopy and locked it. How could I not know that. I should be charged with first-degree stupidity.'

'I'm still not sure what you're talking about?'

'You locked the canopy fully closed – remember – to be on the safe side… with the notebook and the tools.'

'Oh yeah… I do remember that.'

'Well, as a result, the batteries have been recharging ever since. It looks like you fixed the problem without noticing. And the most amazing thing of all is, there's a good chance we'll be going home today.'

'Oh Toby, do you really think so? Do you really *really* think so?'

Toby reached over and put his arm around Sally's shoulder.

'Maybe we should try it now, Sal – what do you think? Should we give it a go?'

'I think... I think we should wait.' Sally advised, staring hard at the machine. 'We've already been down this road, Toby. And I don't think I could handle another disappointment like that. So let's not rush things. Let's just give the batteries the time they need.'

'Yes, yes, of course, you're right as usual. The sensible thing to do is *not* to rush things,' Toby nodded in agreement. 'We should head over to the Globe as planned and try to take our minds off this.'

'We should also go to the Globe, Toby: because it might be the very last time we'll see our friends.'

28. ALL'S WELL THAT ENDS WELL

The Globe was a hive of activity – actors, tradesmen, stagehands and food sellers, all were scrambling about in hectic preparations for the grand opening.

'I still can't believe Hemlock is gone for good,' Growler Mullion was saying to Inky. 'It feels like we've been waiting all our lives for this.'

Toby and Sally smiled at each other.

'Which is why we should enjoy today,' Inky said. 'With that thought in mind, we're off to the top balcony. Everyone is up there, even my mum; it'll be great fun. Do please come and join us, you two.'

'Later maybe,' Sally said tactfully. 'We're hoping to catch Mr. S first.'

'No problem. See you later, then.' Inky smiled, already scampering up the balcony stairs.

'It's hard to imagine that could be the last conversation we'll ever have with him.' Toby said gloomily.

'Yeah, I was thinking that. *Not* joining them feels right – don't you think, Toby.'

Toby nodded. 'Absolutely. It's like everything that's happening right up to this minute is meant to be happening.'

'I know what you mean. Fate is still playing with our lives, in a good way.'

'I think it is too: in a good way.' Toby agreed. 'But I have a teensy bit of a problem, that I'm hoping you can help me with?'

'Sure, what's up?'

'Well… like…. the thing is, I'm not a hundred per cent sure what the play is about? Actually to be honest, I haven't a clue.'

Sally was horrified. 'I don't believe you sometimes, Toby. You've been working with the writer for weeks. How can you *not* know what the play is about?'

'I know, I know, unforgivable and all that. But I was kind of busy with stuff. Like stopping you getting killed and saving the Globe.'

'O-kaaaay. Maybe you did have some extra-weird stuff going on.'

'So maybe I deserve a quick little explanation?' Toby said pleadingly.

Sally sat Toby into a corner and calmly outlined the plot of *The Winter's Tale*. Three minutes later, Toby smiled approvingly.

'Cool. I think I have it. Because of mad jealously this King Leontes dude orders his baby daughter to be dumped and his wife to die in prison. Except she doesn't really die, she just pretends. Lots of weird stuff happens then, until in the last act, when the whole show ends-up all happy-clappy. I guess it's sort of about loss and second chances. A bit like real life, only in reverse.'

Sally frowned and tut-tutted. 'A tad over-simplified, but good enough to see you through.'

Just then, Burbage came rushing from the back of the stage.

'Attention, everybody please, attention. Because of failing light we can't wait any longer, and will have to start without William.'

Sally and Toby watched in awe as the big entry doors swung open, and literally thousands of paying regulars rushed forward. Ten minutes later every square inch of the Globe was crammed with excited, shouty, play-loving Londoners.

To a deluge of whoops and cheers Mr. Burbage made a grandiose stage entrance, bowing to the audience and twirling his hands in a complicated flutter.

'My lords, ladies, gentlemen and others,' he boomed. 'Thank you most sincerely for your esteemed presence at the Globe theatre this fine day. Without further ado I hope you all enjoy the first ever performance of *The Winter's Tale.*'

Bowing extravagantly as he backed away, Burbage then heralded the intro cue. '…enter Archidamus and Camillo!'

One hour later, at the first intermission, the audience erupted into tumultuous applause. Nobody applauded louder than a man hidden away at the back.

'Mr. S, he made it!' Sally squealed, waving her arms like a human windmill.

To an avalanche of hugs and kisses from actors and friends alike, Mr. Shakespeare sauntered around backstage soaking-up the acclaim. As soon as he got the chance, he pulled Toby and Sally aside, clamping his arms tightly around them.

'I hardly know what to say.' Shakespeare said. 'Somehow, with your help, we have managed to transform a deadly beginning into a wonderful ending.'

Almost on cue Burbage came rushing over, his voice buzzing with delight.

'It looks like this is the best opening day we've had in yonks,' he exclaimed. 'The next act is just about to start. You should take your seats.'

Toby and Sally looked sadly at each other. Now that their longed-for return home was within reach, they felt awful about it. Mr. Shakespeare watched sympathetically as Toby stared at the ground, shifted uneasily from foot-to-foot, took a deep breath and then stared up at the sky. Sally, meanwhile, had covered her mouth with her hand and started crying softly.

'It's always a tricky affair when leaving friends and loved ones.' Mr. Shakespeare lamented, his hands clasped his behind his back. 'It is even trickier when you are unable to give a reason for your departure. Not wanting to hurt people's feelings is a major difficulty, while at the same time doing what you must do.'

He looked kindly at Toby and Sally. 'I gather you are leaving us.'

Toby exhaled a long quivering breath. 'We found out this morning that we must return home. The news came out of the blue, and to be honest we don't have much choice in the matter.'

'There is no need for explanations. I always knew there was more to you and Sally than meets the eye. No doubt your reasons for secrecy are well founded. So then, you are returning home to York, or is it Bradford perhaps?'

Sally and Toby lowered their heads contritely.

'We're going to miss you all terribly…' Sally began, before breaking off into tears again.

'Worry not, my young friends. I will explain to everybody and make them understand. And you never know, we might meet again sometime in the future. For now though, farewell, and thank you for all you have done for us.'

The second act was starting as Mr. Shakespeare turned and walked out of their lives forever. Sally directed her teary gaze towards the balcony where Inky and Herbert were joking around with Mincer, Stinky, and Growler, and a smiling Mrs. Blyster. Sid was also there, laughing hysterically, his shoulder wrapped in a cotton sling. It was the happiest Toby and Sally had ever seen him.

Catching a casual wave from Inky, Toby waved back. Sally kissed the air and blew it towards them. With tears streaming down both their faces, they linked arms and headed for Puddle Street.

29. THE BIG SWITCHEROO

The fear that something might still go unfixably wrong filled Sally with a horrible empty feeling. It was so horrible, even as she put one foot on the bottom stair, she stopped.

'Sally, it'll be ok.' Toby smiled reassuringly. 'I can feel it in my bones.'

'I sure hope your bones are up to the job!' she said nervously. 'Ok then, let's go.'

An icy wind whistled down the hall as they slowly walked up the stairs and entered the attic. Even then, Sally was reluctant to approach the Mark 5.

'I can't, Toby, it's all too much,' she said helplessly, wiping her sweaty palms on her jeans. 'Please, you check it… on your own.'

'Sure. You just wait right here.'

Sally gazed at the mattresses and the candles and all the other bits and bobs scattered around the attic, like scraps of memory waiting to be forgotten. Outside, snow was starting to fall, covering the city in white silence. Sally shivered.

'It's all looks ok!' Toby exclaimed with a smile. 'The grid is fully charged and ready to go.'

Sally walked slowly towards the cockpit of the Mark 5.

'See, told you!' Toby smiled, nodding towards the control panel.

Sally looked inside. The grid lights were ablaze.

'Oh Toby. I can hardly believe this is happening, and it really *is* happening, right?'

'Yes, Sally. It really is happening.'

Grabbing a final look around the little attic, they carefully climbed into the snug cockpit of the Mark 5. Without dithering or hesitating Toby pulled the canopy down, locked it securely into place, and held his finger over the big red switch. He turned to Sally and smiled confidently.

'Right. Here goes.'

He flicked the big red switch, sat back, and they both held their breaths.

For one interminably long stretched-out minute nothing happened.

'Oh no, not again,' Sally whimpered, holding her hands to her forehead. 'It's like a non-stop nightmare!'

And still they waited….and waited…. and just when they were on the verge of being totally crushed by disappointment, a blinding burst of flashing lights and a shuddering jolt raced through the machine.

It was marvellous and amazing and fantastic. Toby and Sally screamed with delight as the noise and the smoke got louder and louder, until finally…

'FFFFFUUMPH!'

…they were off again! And almost as quickly as the mad hullabaloo started – it was over.

EPILOGUE

Almost as soon as Toby and Sally had disappeared, the professor started working on his computers. He was desperately urgently trying to figure-out what had happened, what had gone so catastrophically wrong. So totally focused was he on his work he hardly noticed the beads of sweat trickling down his forehead, or the police helicopter thundering across the rooftops, or anything else for that matter. Every so often he thought about standing up to squeeze the stiffness out of his joints, maybe even put the kettle on for a cup of tea. But just as quickly he carried-on working, worrying and investigating.

All of a sudden that awful juddering and shaking started up again. Bits of roof plaster began to rain down in a spattering of clips and clacks. In terror the professor dropped to the floor again and pulled his white coat over his head.

For a few heart-stopping moments the noise got louder and louder and scarier and scarier. Then, just like before, it all stopped – and again that most peculiar noise spluffed through the attic...

'FFFF F*UUMPH!'*

...it went, followed by a long eerie silence?

When the professor peeked out from his coat, he almost passed out with relief. The Mark 5 had mysteriously reappeared!

'Please-oh-please let this be the right place,' a disembodied voice called through the hazy smoke. 'Unc? Uncle Arthur? Are you there?'

'Great scot, Toby. It that you?' The professor shouted back.

And sure enough, standing right there in front of him, alive and well, was his wonderful beloved nephew. To make sure he wasn't imagining things, the professor grabbed Toby and started patting him up and down. 'You really are here, right?'

With arms and legs all over the place, a pair of laughing Sprockets began dancing and bopping around the attic. With his mental state rapidly returning to normal, the professor couldn't help noticing certain changes in his nephew.

'Good heavens,' he said, his bushy eyebrows shooting halfway up his forehead. 'You *do* look odd!' He then sniffed at Toby's head. 'And you smell like an old sock. I very much hope Sally has fared better?'

On cue, coughing and flapping through the smoke, Sally came into view.

'My dear child,' the professor began sorrowfully. 'I am truly sorry for the fright you must have....'

The words froze in his mouth. He did a double-take. For instead of finding a pretty-faced Sally Bunn: a tatty Sally with pale skin, sunken cheeks and a mass of electrocuted hair was stood there. Staring stupidly, the professor flopped down onto a chair.

'Y-your hair. I don't--'

'...do *not* get me started on my hair,' Sally calmly interrupted the professor. 'We're lucky to be alive and it's all the fault of that crazy machine of yours.'

The professor had heard enough, and before another

word was spoken he rushed to the bank of computers and began jabbing at a keyboard.

'There... that's it... it's over,' he declared, as the Mark 5 stuttered and sputtered and finally plinked out altogether. 'I've turned the whole thing off.'

'That's great, Unc. It really is,' said Toby, leaning down and staring into his uncle's face. 'But there's something we really need to know?'

'Of course, just ask.'

'Exactly how long have we been away?'

'Let me think now. Yes... well...at the very most I would say you were gone for six, maybe even seven minutes.'

Marshalling his thoughts, Toby crouched down beside his uncle.

'Well, the thing is, Unc. We weren't away for six or seven minutes. We were away for two terrifying weeks. And this Anti-Gravity machine of yours. It's not an Anti-anything. It is in fact a fully functional, fully operational, time machine. And Sally is absolutely right. It very nearly got us both killed.'

The professor's first reaction were to shout balderdash and baloney. But something held him back. His eyes swivelled from Toby to Sally and to the Mark 5. There was no doubting the changes in the teenager's appearance. And he saw for himself how the Mark 5 mysteriously disappeared and then reappeared. But a time machine?

He smiled sympathetically. 'Toby, lad. I have no doubt you and Sally have been through a traumatic experience. But time machines don't exist. In Star Trek, yes. But in real life... can't happen.'

Despite the professor's objections, Sally could see a spark of uncertainty hiding behind his eyes.

'Eh, excuse me, professor?' she said quietly. 'I know something that could change your mind. It's down in the little cubbyhole.'

Toby's eyes lit-up. 'The names! You're right, Sal. I forgot all about the names. Please Unc, come down now to the cubbyhole. You have to see this… we *all* have to see it!!'

The professor sighed heavily. 'Alright, Toby. But I'm warning you. If this is some kind of joke…'

Toby grabbed a small torch from the professor's bench and ushered him down the stairs. A minute later they were crawling through the cubbyhole.

'Ok Unc, remember the old names – Herbert Herring and Inky Blyster?'

'Of course, I remember. I'm hardly likely to forget.'

'Well then… take a look now.'

Toby flashed a light at the far wall. The professor crawled in for a closer look.

Herbert Herring
Toby Sprocket (Hi Unc!)
Inky Blyster
1610

Holding his breath, he stared goggle-eyed at the wall. It was like Toby had magically pulled an elephant out of his pocket.

'T-That's impossible!' he stuttered, touching the words Hi Unc! with trembling fingers. 'I swear, Toby. If you've been messing around with that inscription, I won't be responsible for my actions.'

'Unc, believe me. I haven't been messing around with anything. Nor is this some stupid joke. You created a time machine, and I wrote my name on that wall in the year 1610.'

In his wildest dreams the professor could not imagine such a thing. Yet, here in a dusty little cubbyhole, was clear evidence that something truly amazing had happened. The very idea was dizzying. Even as he sat there on that dusty floor, ideas swarmed around his head, and billions of brain cells fired-off facts and figures. "Hadn't Einstein himself study time travel?" he thought. In fact, according to his $E = mc^2$ equation, time travel was theoretically possible, at least in one direction, towards the future. He put a trembling hand to his mouth.

'This is totally remarkable. I don't know what to say. I-I mean I literally do not know what to say. And these "two terrifying weeks" what exactly happened to you?'

It was only when Toby and Sally tried to gather their thoughts and to recount what had happened, did the sheer terrifying weirdness of it all begin to hit home. For a few utterly confusing seconds they just stood staring at each other.

Eventually they managed to begin their story, and for about thirty minutes, without stopping once, they recounted the most extraordinary tale the professor had ever heard.

It could have been the re-telling of what happened or it could have been just seeing the professor again. Whatever it was, Toby and Sally were suddenly desperate to get outdoors to see and feel and smell the streets they had missed so much.

'Unc, like... Can we talk later? We kinda need to make sure that this really is a dream come true and not just the start of another nightmare.'

'Of course, yes, I understand,' the professor said. 'The wheel of fate has come full circle. I've only been waiting for six minutes, so I suppose another few minutes won't kill me. The story will sound an awful lot better with time. Off you go then. Enjoy the moment.'

Charging downstairs and then outside like a pair of demented terriers, they slammed the front door so hard the entire house shook.

Finally, at long long last, with hearts pounding and eyes ready to burst into tears, they were dancing in the middle of good old Puddle Street, sucking-in the energy of their London. Buses… jets… sirens… honking cars… smiley tourists taking photos of two crazy teenagers dancing in front of honking cars … the ka-thump of those same honking cars rear-ending each other. Nothing but nothing could stop their celebrations.

Happy beginnings and happy endings stretched away in every direction from Toby and Sally. Less than an hour earlier they were trembling with fear of never seeing this again. Now they were home, in their right place, and everything was normal and beautiful and brilliant.

The End?

Acknowledgements

With sincere thanks to all of those who have encouraged and supported my work: Mary Morrissy, Dr. Eibhear Walsh (Creative Writing Programme, Department of English, University College Cork), Sydney Landon Plum and Susanne Davis (Faculty in Creative Writing, University of Connecticut), Caoimhe Young (Magazine Editor, *Sunday World*), Ellis Delmonte (Publisher, Hawkwood Books).

Particular thanks to my wife, Marie, my siblings and their families (too many mention individually) and friends Andrea Ainsworth, Andy Crook, Martin Drury and Sharon Murphy.

About the author

Alan Kelly was born in Dublin and raised in Leixlip, Co. Kildare (Ireland). He has a BA Arts (Intl.) from University College Dublin and the University of Connecticut (USA) and an MA Creative Writing from University College Cork. Since 2012 he has been known to readers in Ireland as the restaurant reviewer of the *Sunday World* newspaper, writing under the pseudonym of 'Grub Spy'. He currently lives in Cork City and writes fiction for young people and adults. This is Alan's first novel.